THE GATHERING ROOM

The

Gathering Room

Colby Rodowsky

FARRAR · STRAUS · GIROUX

New York

Library of Congress Cataloging in Publication Data
Rodowsky, Colby F.
The gathering room.
[1. Family life—Fiction.   2. Cemeteries—Fiction.
3. Aunts—Fiction]   I. Title.
PZ7.R6185Gat   [Fic]   81-5360
ISBN 0-374-32520-0   AACR2

For Larry, again, with love

THE GATHERING ROOM

The windows on the street side of the house have a closed look that stretches from day to day, and month to month, almost as far back as anyone cares to remember.

The house itself is made of stone, and mossed around the bottom. It spans the driveway, arching over the road in a curve that somehow shapes itself into a room bridging the two parts of the house.

The greater part of the house is on the left of the drive, jumbled there like a small fortress, with turrets and casement windows and cubbyholes. In this, the larger side, is the living room, where the floorboards are wide and the window glass is thick and whorled. Behind this, through a narrow hall that is lined on both sides with Ned's books, is the kitchen. The kitchen floor is brick, worn smooth in places, and it dips down by the back door and at the foot of the stairs. In the summer, when Serena takes up the rag rugs, the floor gives the house a cool and slightly damp feeling.

The stairs from the kitchen lead to the second floor: to the bedrooms. The one belonging to Mudge is small, as is the spare room—there has never been a visitor to make it a guest room. But the largest, by far, is the room in the archway that connects the two parts of the house. Dropping down from the corner of this room—Serena's room, and Ned's—is a narrow, circular staircase that leads to the gathering room.

The gathering room is the right side of the house.

The house is a gatehouse. And there are, in fact, large, black gates that shut with a terrible clang when Ned pulls them closed every night.

The house is a sentinel: welcoming, guarding, and watching over the whole of Edgemount Cemetery.

It is the link that joins the walls on either side of the driveway: walls that are high and netted over with vines.

And on the outside, just beyond the walls, swarming and teeming and swirling around them, is the city. The city comes so close it touches the edge of the wall: touches it with dirt that blows from the street, with old newspapers and flattened paper cups that tangle in the vines, with bus transfers and beer cans and shards of broken glass that clump together and rim the bottom of it. The city comes so close it breathes exhaust fumes from buses and taxis and moving vans. It slams against the walls and over the top and into Edgemount with the sound of horns and brakes and sirens, of whistles and car doors and children crying and fighting and playing in the street. The city comes so close that its houses and stores and taverns line the streets, jammed one on top of the other, centering in on Edgemount like spokes of a wheel.

But the gatehouse, the sentinel, the link in the wall, stands impassively—and on the street side the shades are drawn.

1

Mudge stood at the back window of the gathering room and waited for Ned to come home. He pressed his forehead against the glass and looked up the road, sensing rather than feeling the wind. The stones, the monuments, even the angels wielding swords, seemed to draw in upon themselves, taking their color from the leaden sky overhead. The windowpane rattled and Mudge pressed harder against it, as if by quieting it he could still the wind outside. He wished that his father would come down from the hill where he had gone to repair a gate. He wished that the snow, if it was going to start, would come.

Behind him the room was warm, and Mudge heard the wood crackling in the stove. He saw, without turning to look at them, his books jumbled on the trestle table. Saw the open atlas and his paper and colored pencils and knew that he should get back to the map that Ned had left for him to do. He saw, without looking, Ned's and Serena's guitars leaning on either side of the window seat, and faintly, from somewhere inside of him, he heard the tracings of the songs they sang together: of "Barbara Allen," and "Lonesome Valley," of "John Peel" and "Down by the Sally Gardens."

But Mudge knew it was more than the after-sounds of the songs that made the gathering room special. More than the warmth of the stove and the guitars, more even than the plat that hung on the wall, marking Edgemount into sections and the sections into lots.

It was a presence, a crowding: an imprint left on the room, the way leaves stay and mark themselves upon the ground. It was a gathering.

Mudge knew, watching from the window as the first flurries of snow drove down, that the room had been built as a waiting place. He knew that in the early 1800's, when travel was poor and roads were long, there had to be a place for mourners to come together, to gather, waiting for one another and for a funeral to begin. That was in the time when Edgemount was new and far beyond the city; before the city pushed and hunched its way upon it and circled the outside wall like a mural.

It was as though the room still contained that waiting and held it there. And the men and women, the mourners, peopled Mudge's world as his friends up on the hill did—Dorro and the Judge and the Butterfly Lady. As Serena and Ned did. And this peopling overlapped like circles in the water that widened and spiraled when Mudge dropped stones into the pond.

Mudge still watched from the window as the rosebushes, overgrown and rangy now, twisted in the wind. He sensed the crowd in back of him in the empty room: the people from time past: years gone by. It was as though he saw them superimposed on the window glass, at once magnified and diminished. He saw the women in their capes and mourning bonnets lining the benches; the men pacing the floor, their boots scraping against the stones. There was a shuffling, a waiting, an expectation.

Mudge turned from the window and went back to the table. He traced the route of the Underground Railroad on the map in red, then dropped the pencil and watched it roll across the table and fall to the floor. He made no effort to pick it up, but sat with his chin cupped in his hand and tried to sort the sounds and silences around him.

Yet there was a restless feeling about this day, and for once Mudge didn't feel at home in the gathering room. The threat of snow had hung over them all morning, and instead of the usual lessons, Ned had gone up the hill to repair the gate on the Nickerson vault, to keep it from clanking in the wind. The sky had seemed low enough to touch when Serena had gone off to the store, hurrying down the street with her dark braid caught up in a wool cap and her shoulders hunched against the wind.

Mudge went to the outside door and listened, hoping to hear his mother coming back, her cart bumping against the cobblestones. He waited to see if he could hear her unlocking the front door on the other side of the drive.

Instead, he heard the silence of the snow and the ticking

of the clock. The room had a sudden empty feeling. At the same time, crosshatched against the emptiness was a sense of intrusion. It was as though something had come into the room and jolted it. Instinctively, Mudge took hold of either side of the table, though he knew the jolting was not a physical thing: that it came from something that went below the surface.

Then Mudge remembered the letter.

And in the remembering he wondered how he could have forgotten it: letters didn't come often to Edgemount. There were the occasional ones asking the whereabouts of a relative, an ancestor, and Serena would locate them on the plat and would write answers from her desk in the corner of the gathering room. Sometimes there were letters from people who wanted to be buried there, and Serena would write back and say there was no longer room for anyone to come to Edgemount to stay. Every once in a while, there were letters asking about old monuments or unusual markers; at times, there were envelopes marked "Occupants," containing coupons for soap and syrup and breakfast cereal.

There were never letters for Ned and Serena and Mudge.

The letter had come just after Ned had left to go up the hill; after Serena had gone to the store. It came while Mudge was doing the dishes, just when he had smeared a clear place in the steamed-up window and stood staring out at the remains of Serena's cabbage and cauliflower patch.

The letter came with a rush of cold air through the slot in the door, and landed with a slap on the rag rug.

Mudge finished the dishes, watching the garden disappear as the window over the sink steamed up again. He dried his hands and picked up the letter, ready to toss it on the kitchen table.

The envelope was heavy and square, with his father's name in stubby letters on the front. The handwriting drew Mudge's attention with the insistence of someone tapping a stick sharply against the floor, and Mudge weighed the letter first in one hand and then in the other. He read the name in the upper left-hand corner: Ernestus Stokes.

Ernestus Stokes. He was Stokes: Mudge Stokes. And Serena and Ned were Stokes. Ned and Serena and Mudge Stokes. It was the name Ernestus that jarred against him. And he remembered it in the niggling way of things he wanted to forget: his half year in kindergarten, and a street with children on it, and buses and cars and taxis, and, once, a trip to the circus. Mudge remembered all these things and knew they were from that parcel of time before they came to live at Edgemount: before Ned pruned the bushes and fixed broken gates and went out rarely, walking into the center of the city—to the library—and coming home with a canvas sack of books slung on his back. Before Serena rode the tractor and cut the grass and went alone through the streets to the store. Before they moved to Edgemount.

Mudge had put the letter on the table, propped against the yellow sugar bowl, and gone along to the other side of the house to wait for the snow and to trace the Underground Railroad on the map with a red pencil.

But the red pencil still lay on the floor and the thought of the name grew and surged through the house and pushed at the presence in the gathering room: at the mourners who lined the bench: at the echo of Ned's songs, and Serena's. The fire in the wood stove burned low and the room was chill.

Mudge jumped up, pushing the chair over in back of him and sending it clattering to the floor. He ran up the stairs, circling around and around, through his parents' room, and down into the kitchen.

The letter still leaned propped against the sugar bowl, and though Mudge was surprised to see that it was no larger than an ordinary envelope, he still felt a kind of insistence about it. He had the same jolting feeling that he had had in the gathering room: as though things were rearranging themselves beneath him.

He dug his jacket out of the cupboard and put it on, shoving his arms down into the sleeves, and pulling his gloves out of the pockets. Grabbing the letter, he threw open the door and ran outside.

Mudge stopped for a moment and let the wind and snow drive against him. The snow stung his face and he blinked quickly. He felt his hair frosting over and his lashes were rimmed with white. Stepping off the porch, he planted his feet in the snow, lifting them out carefully, taking several deliberate giant steps.

Then Mudge started to run. He slipped and slid, going down first on one knee and then the other. He worked his way onto the grass and started up the hill. "Ned . . . Ned . . ." he called.

Mudge ran past the fork in the road that led to the gazebo. He caught himself on a wrought-iron fence, and inched his way along past a granite angel holding a scroll. He pushed himself down into the gully by the side of the road where he could get a better foothold. He brushed the top of his head and wished that he had worn a hat.

He stood where the road curved up past the vaults and looked back the way he had come, watching the footprints of his tennis shoes being swallowed by the snow. He turned back, his head down, his body slanting into the wind, and started up blindly, walking smack into Ned.

"Whoa, where're you going?" said Ned, catching hold of Mudge's shoulder. "I was just on my way down."

"We got a letter, Ned. We got a letter."

"People do," said Ned, turning Mudge around and starting down the hill.

"We don't."

"Well, we could. I mean, it's not . . ."

"It says 'Ernestus,'" said Mudge, holding the envelope out to his father. "Ernestus Stokes. Ernestus . . . Ernestus . . . ErnestusErnestusErnestus." Mudge held the word and swung it around, like a trick with a basket of eggs that Ned had shown him once—somehow knowing that if he stopped, bits of the world, like the eggs, would come crashing down around him.

"Ernestus," his father whispered in a puff of cold white air that was quieter than the snow that fell around them.

"Ernestus," he said out loud, grabbing the envelope out of Mudge's hand and starting down the hill. "How dare she . . . no right . . . told her once and for all . . ." The words, hurled over Ned's shoulder, stung Mudge full in the face as he went slipping and sliding after his father down the hill.

2

"It's a letter from Ernestus," said Ned as he threw open the back door and saw Serena unpacking groceries at the kitchen table.

"Oh, Ned—how did she . . . what . . ." She came around the table, holding a box of crackers. "Did she say how she found us—how she . . ."

Mudge took off his coat and dropped it on a chair, then stood with his back pressed against the door, feeling the crosspieces of the panes digging into his back, and the wisps of cold air seeping into the room. He watched his father shrug out of his coat; saw the snow on his red hair and beard disappear in a series of tiny explosions. He saw his father's hand shake as he tore open the envelope and began to read out loud.

Brother,

It has been a long time. A long, long time. When you left I looked for you (you must know how I looked)—but after a while there was nothing to do but go on with my life, which

is what—at the time—I tried to convince you must be done.
But I went on always with an ear tuned for your whereabouts;
always with a hope of hearing from you.

Recently I read an article that was carried in our local paper
about the efforts to make Edgemount Cemetery a Historic
Site. And in that article the writer mentioned the caretaker's
son by name—and that name was Mudge (there're not that
many of them). I began to investigate.

And now I've found you.

When John Gordon was killed, you said I did not under-
stand your grief—your way of handling things. I only under-
stand what Mama and Papa taught me: what I, in turn, tried
to teach you. That we must face what has to be faced.

And now that I have found you I am coming to Edge-
mount: to see you, and to see Serena. To see Mudge and to
meet his friends and see where he goes to school. Because,
like you and Serena, he is a part of me.

I am coming and will not be put off.

Until then,

Ernestus

"She's coming here. Ernestus is coming here," said Ned,
moving forward to sit down at the table.

"But think how she must feel," Serena said. "Finding us
after all these years."

"We weren't lost."

"She didn't know where we were . . . hasn't known these
many years," said Serena, filling the kettle and putting it on
the stove.

"We knew," said Ned in a thin voice. "Just because people choose to leave, to disappear, doesn't mean they're lost."

Mudge ached with the stiffness of holding himself against the door. He wanted to dash across the room and up the stairs, away from the words he did not understand. He wanted to get away from the idea of Aunt Ernestus, who was coming here because of seeing his name in a story he had not even known existed.

"Maybe it will be all right," said Serena, turning back to the table. "Especially for Mudge . . . never known any family . . . an aunt might be . . ."

"Oh, come off it, Serena," said Ned, slamming his fist onto the table and making the sugar bowl jump and the letter topple forward. "We're his family—all the family he needs. She ought to stay where she is, where she belongs. It's like a plague of locusts—and like the locusts, there's nothing we can do." He pushed his chair back, scraping it angrily against the floor.

Mudge heard Ned go through the hall and into the living room. He heard the front door slam, and then, seconds later, the muffled slam of the gathering-room door sounding like an echo.

And Mudge felt as though he had to escape. "I'm going out," he said, jumping away from the door and letting his breath whoosh out all at once.

"Oh, Mudge," said Serena, swinging around to face him. "I didn't know . . . forgot you were . . ."

Mudge scrabbled in the cupboard under the stairs, searching for his boots. He heard Serena's voice calling to him through the tangle of scarves and coats that webbed his head.

"Do you have to? Go out, I mean. With the weather and . . ."

Mudge crawled backward out of the cupboard. "Aw, Serena, you know I've got to go. Got to see them." He shoved his left foot down into his black rubber boot and pulled, struggling to get it over his wet tennis shoe. "Got to see Dorro 'cause I said I would if it snowed, and the Captain, I guess, because I'll be up that way, except the cold makes his joints ache and then he blames it on Jenkins. He blames everything on Jenkins. And then the Judge, but not Frieda—she laughs at things. I'll start with the Butterfly Lady. I always do when it's important. And end with the Nickersons, because there're so many of them and they know about aunts and relatives and stuff." Mudge wished he could pull that last sentence back: stop it before it went spinning across the room between them. Before it reminded Serena of Aunt Ernestus.

"And you don't, do you? Know about aunts and relatives and stuff, I mean." Serena moved the teapot that was whistling shrilly and turned back to look at her son for a long time. "Oh, Mudge, come and sit for a minute. We have to talk. You can't go running off as though nothing had happened."

"Ser-en-a," said Mudge, stepping forward as though he were playing Giant Steps. "I've got to go. I told you—to see Dorro and . . ."

"A minute, Mudge."

"No. No minute. Not now. I have to . . ."

"Enough. Enough already," said Serena as she fixed herself a mug of strong black tea. "We have to talk—about things that happened before we came to Edgemount. There must be things you remember. Things you want to ask about."

"No. No, Serena. Honest. I don't remember anything. It's all just here. This house and the pond and the gathering room."

"Life didn't begin with Edgemount," said Serena, sitting down and indicating a chair to Mudge. "There were all those years before, and maybe we've spent so much time going forward that we haven't taken the time to turn around and see where we've been. Maybe that's what we have to do now."

And suddenly it was as though something had given way and Mudge was five years old again and out of kindergarten for the afternoon. It was January and cold, and a sharp wind caught the flags and buntings around the State House and made them snap. There were chairs on the frozen, bumpy ground and State Troopers lined down the steps and along the speaker's platform. There were signs leading to special seating and Serena edging him along and all the while the two of them searching through the crowd for Ned. There was band music. And drums that made his insides ache. Serena had pulled Mudge close and enfolded him in her coat. He could still smell the warm wool of her coat; could still feel the satin lining cool against his cheek.

Mudge wanted to bury himself in Serena's coat again and wrap it tight around him.

And Mudge remembered in spite of himself. In spite of

tunneling under things and burrowing deep inside; of turning and running the other way and holding his ears and covering his eyes. In spite of it all, Mudge remembered. And the remembering ached somewhere deep inside of him.

It had happened when the governor had stepped to the front of the platform to begin his speech. Mudge and Serena had been in the special chairs just below the speaker's platform, behind the scarlet ribbon. Mudge remembered how the chair had wobbled and how he had kicked the back of the seat in front of him because his feet didn't reach the ground and how he had scrunched down to see Ned sitting to the right and in back of the governor. Mudge had shoved his mittened hands down in his pockets and tried to make his father look at him by staring hard.

The shot came just when Mudge managed to get his father's attention and for a moment they stared at one another as if they couldn't let each other go, and Mudge saw a horror deep inside Ned's eyes. And then there wasn't any more to see because the troopers stepped forward and linked themselves around the platform, and even the people in the special seating were pushed back into the crowd.

"We went to a hotel, didn't we," said Mudge, slumping into his chair. "And sat by the window and watched it get dark and saw the lights go on outside—down below. And I got hold of Oscar the monkey and held him till his stuffings ached."

"Oh, yes," said Serena, smiling. "There was Oscar the monkey."

But Mudge wasn't listening: was thinking instead of the funny floppy monkey with the green velvet pants and cap and a flattened face. Of the monkey he had held to go to sleep at night and when the world rocked beneath him. Of the same monkey, more faded now, shoved on the back of the shelf over his bed behind an old, no longer used fire truck and a half-finished model plane. The same monkey that he sometimes reached out to touch with one finger on his way in or out of the room: quickly, so no one would see.

"And there was something about a flag, before that," said Mudge, running his finger along the inside of his scarf. "I'm not sure what."

"It was the flag in the town square. We could see it from the hotel, and someone went out and lowered it halfway, and that's how we knew the governor was dead."

"And we waited there a long time without turning any lights on . . . Until Ned came back and we went home. And Ned cared awfully, didn't he, Serena?"

"He cared awfully. And it was a hard thing to see. And frightening, too."

"Who was he—the governor?"

"He was Ned's friend." And then Serena went on, as though Mudge hadn't spoken. "The thing about Ned is that he has always been an alone kind of person—and that's all right. But sometimes they are the ones most easily hurt. When John decided to run for governor on an anti-corruption platform, it meant a lot to Ned, and he threw himself in whole hog. Maybe for the first time in his life. It was a beautiful thing to see, and when the shooting happened, it wasn't just John Gordon who was killed—but some new beginning part of Ned."

"But what's it all got to do with Aunt Ernestus? With her coming here?"

Serena made herself another cup of tea, then waited until it was well steeped and she had dropped the tea bag into the trash. "Afterward, after it was all done—the funeral and the winding up—then Ned just went home. Away from the office, the law. Away from everything except you and me. And at the time that's all he could do."

"That's when we came here?"

"Yes, I found this. Because we needed something to ourselves. For Ned's sake. And it's been good. But it was never meant to be a permanent thing. In fact, if the Historic Preservationists have their way, all of Edgemount, and the house as well, will be declared a Historic Site. It's been dragging on for years—largely a matter of money. But a few years ago when we thought of leaving, thought maybe we'd been here long enough, the Trustees asked us to stay on until everything was settled. Rather than get somebody new . . . and then things just seemed to drift along, the way things do. But that's okay, because it's been good here. That must have been what Aunt Ernestus saw an article about in her paper."

"But about Aunt Ernestus . . ."

"Yes—about Ernestus. She was the only family that either one of us had, and she was pretty rough. She badgered. She lectured. She . . . But no, that's not a fair way to start," said Serena, tilting her mug and watching the tea rise and fall against the side. "There are some things you have to understand about Ernestus.

"She is Ned's sister, but she's old enough to be his mother. She was twenty-seven when Ned was born. It was always Ernestus who did all the mother things, and the father things as well."

"But what about his real parents—Ned's mother and father—my gr-grandparents . . ." And Mudge fumbled over the word as though he had never pronounced it before.

"They were there—but in the background mostly. His mother was sickly and his father worked on the railroad. They were only too happy to leave him to Ernestus. And it was Ernestus who told him stories and took him places. It was Ernestus who . . . After their mother died and their father became an invalid, Ernestus just kept right on—caring for him and doing for Ned. And by the time he was ten, both of his real parents were dead, but life was going on pretty much as usual."

"But not to have any parents . . ." Mudge dug his fingers into the undersides of his legs.

"But, in a sense, Ernestus *was* his parents. They used to do wonderful things together, go places. And after Ned grew up, she just kept right on caring for others—used to go out as a kind of practical nurse. 'See if you can get Ernestus Stokes' is what people said when there was trouble."

"But then why . . . I don't understand—about Ned and after his friend was killed," said Mudge.

Serena got up and went to stand by the door, looking out and tracing her fingers over the condensation on the glass.

"Well, right at that time, Ned felt that he needed to back off from things. It was as though his world was coming apart and he had to get away from everything and everybody in it. This was his way of dealing with things—and about all I could do was to help him handle it in his own way: give him that freedom. But Ernestus had raised him, had put him through law school, and somehow she couldn't bear to see him give it up. It finally got to the point that we just had to leave where we were, without telling anyone. Left and came here.

". . . the thing about Ernestus, I guess you'd say, is that she's a one-way kind of person," Serena went on. "Seeing something the way it should be, and that's all there is to it. No ifs, ands, or buts. But most of us can't manage to see things quite so simply—or to do it even if we do see it. I still remember her saying, 'You do what you have to do,' until I thought I'd . . ."

"You do what you have to do . . . You do what you have to do . . . You do what you have to do . . ." Mudge heard Serena say the words, and layered somewhere in back of his mother's voice he heard Aunt Ernestus saying them herself. "You do what you have to do . . ." Over and over and over again.

The words thundered through the house; but it was a different house. They pulsed their way up the stairs and under the door and into his room; but it was a different room.

"You do what you have to do . . ."

The words exploded into a strong white light that glared down at Mudge and left him no place to hide.

He looked around wildly, shaking his head and pushing his hands against the tabletop; seeing, as if from a distance, Serena watching him.

"Mudge, what's wrong—what—you look funny . . . as if . . ." And her face that had been large and had filled all the spaces around him seemed to recede to its normal size.

"It was just that I remembered things—saw them, sort of—when you said that about Aunt Ernestus."

"What things, Mudge?" asked Serena, coming to stand in back of Mudge and putting her hands on his shoulders. "What things?"

"Nothing much. Just stuff and . . . it doesn't matter." Mudge squirmed under Serena's hands, but she held them firm for a moment, then moved back to her place on the other side of the table.

"I think it matters—think that this remembering matters very much. If only . . ."

"It's just that afterward—after Ned's friend was killed— well, like you've always said, 'Afterward we just came to Edgemount to live'—the way in a story you would say 'They lived happily ever after.' Only you know there was stuff that happened in between. Things that went on and all, and now it's as though that stuff's just lumping up inside of me."

"And that lumping up hurts some, doesn't it?"

"Well, yeah, I guess. But, hey, Serena—afterward—there *was* stuff that went on, wasn't there? Stuff with Ned?"

Serena pushed her thumbs down inside her fists until her knuckles were an angry red. "Yes, there was stuff with Ned."

"And sometimes he would sit and stare and not say anything at all, and sometimes he would . . . sometimes he would cry . . . out loud, and at night . . ."

"Everyone has to cry, Mudge."

"And one time—the worst time—he cried and cried, a big gulping kind of crying, and he—Ned—came after me and his face was all . . . and he was shaking and . . . and I ran and . . ."

"He just wanted to hold you. To have you hold him . . ."

"But he was my *father*, Serena. For pete's sake, he was my father, and I was . . . I was scared." And Mudge felt as though the words had been wrenched from somewhere deep inside of him. He fell back against the chair, and for a moment the room was silent. Then he went on, almost as though he couldn't stop himself.

"And I ran away. Ran upstairs and into my room and slammed the door and pushed the toy box against it and went to hide under the bed, only after a while I came out because I wanted to hear you when you came."

"Only I didn't come," said Serena, looking right at Mudge, "because there was Ned downstairs and he really needed me right then and . . ."

"It's okay," said Mudge, as if anxious to go on. "And there was other stuff that night. People coming . . . a man . . . and another man . . ."

"A doctor. I had to find a doctor for Ned—and a neighbor, a friend, I called when I didn't know what else to do."

And Mudge seemed to slip back into that other night. It

was as though he were still crouched on top of the toy box in his green-and-yellow striped pajamas, with his face pressed against the cool inside of his bedroom door. He traced the sound of voices—straining when they dropped down low and jerking back when they pulsed out at him. Words about help and hospitals. Hushed words spoken in a monotone. Soothing words. And woven through those words was the sound of someone crying—a racking kind of crying that made Mudge pull his knees up under his chin and dig his fingers into his legs until the skin was numb. And crashing down on top of those other voices, that other sound, was someone saying, "You do what you have to do . . . You do what you have to do . . ."

"She was there that night too, wasn't she?" said Mudge, looking at Serena. "Aunt Ernestus, I mean."

"Yes. Aunt Ernestus was there. She came in just at the very worst moment. We had just begun to get Ned quieted down, had calmed him some and . . . The doctor had thought perhaps some kind of therapy, maybe even a hospital. And there was Ernestus telling him to pull himself together . . . to shape up. As if he wanted to be that way . . . as if . . ."

"You do what you have to do," said Mudge, repeating the refrain of that one particular night. He remembered how the voices had gotten louder and louder, how he had finally opened his bedroom door and let them wash over him. He remembered the sudden stillness as the voices stopped, and after a while the sight of two men he didn't know struggling up the steps with Ned crumpled down between them. It was then that Mudge had closed his door and pushed the toy box back in front of it and had gone silently to bed, pulling the covers up over his head and keeping them there until morning.

"And the next morning," said Mudge, "the next morning it was as though it had never happened. There was Ned sleeping and sleeping . . ."

"The medicine the doctor gave him."

"And when I asked you . . ."

Serena got up and started around the table toward Mudge, then turned back and stood behind her chair, holding on to the wooden slats. "Oh, Mudge, I only wanted to make it all right. Wanted to make everything the way it was, so that when you asked me the next day I said . . ."

"You didn't know. You said you didn't know what I meant. That maybe it was a dream and not to worry about it—that everything was fine."

"I wanted it to be fine—for Ned and for you—for all of us. And after everybody left, after Ned was asleep, and you too, I sat up all night trying to decide what to do. How to help Ned help himself. I knew about this place, the job here, and the house, and I decided we would try it. There wasn't anybody left to ask—I mean, with everybody telling me something different. And then when you asked . . . and I was so tired . . . and I guess I thought if I pretended that everything was all right, it would be."

"Only I knew what I'd heard . . . what I'd seen," Mudge said, more to himself than to Serena. "And for a long time afterward I was afraid to go to sleep at night."

"Oh, Mudge, I am sorry. I wanted to help Ned and . . ."

"But then after we'd been here for a while it got to be okay. And there was the Butterfly Lady and Dorro and the Captain and all those guys . . ."

" . . . never meant to hurt you and somehow I didn't think we'd stay this long," Serena said.

". . . and Ned got to be the way he used to be . . . and there were songs and the stories and the school in the gathering room . . ."

"Maybe we shouldn't have come at all. But somehow I thought that because we all cared about each other so—the three of us—that it would be all right. Maybe we should have . . ."

"For pete's sake, Serena, you're not listening. I said it was okay. Better than okay—being here, I mean. There isn't any place else I'd want to be. Ever—ever," said Mudge, jumping up. "It's just that I don't want *her* to come. Aunt Ernestus. We don't *need* her here. Let her stay where she is. Let her leave us alone." He wound the muffler tight around his neck and over his chin.

"She's coming, Mudge," Serena said. "Aunt Ernestus is coming here—to see Ned and me. To see you and where you go to school and . . ."

"But I go to school here."

"Yes, that's another thing," said Serena. "Aunt Ernestus is a great one for things being the way they ought to be. In fact, you could say she's a stickler."

Suddenly Mudge wanted to be outside: wanted it so much that his feet began to jitter under the table. From the gathering room came the sound of his father singing. Mudge watched Serena for a few moments as she listened to Ned's song, then he turned and tiptoed out the door.

Outside, the snow had stopped and the silence was heavy. Mudge started up the road, forking to the right, toward the gazebo and the Butterfly Lady. He stood for a minute breathing deeply and looking out over Edgemount. He swung his arms in great sweeping arcs and stamped his feet on the snowy ground, but somehow he still felt as though things were intruding from the outside in.

3

"I've got a school, you know—in my head," said Mudge, scraping the snow off the butterfly and settling himself down between the wings. He wedged himself into a comfortable position and propped his feet up on the rock. The cold of the iron burned through his jeans.

"A school, have you? Well, I'm not surprised. Got a lot of things in that head of yours, you have." Mudge watched the Butterfly Lady push the snow off a marble slab and seat herself over the words "Awaiting the early dawn . . ."

She shuddered slightly. "Cold goes right through you."

Mudge looked at the Butterfly Lady in her shapeless Mother Hubbard dress and her sensible brown shoes, with her hair in a thick bun at the back of her neck.

"I never thought about the cold and you. I mean, you never said it bothered you. Now, with the Captain, I know—says it makes his joints ache and brings on the misery," said Mudge, shaking his head and wondering what the Butterfly Lady would do if he were to whip off his muffler and wind it around her.

"Hummph. Captain's a complainer, from what you say. A little cold is all it is."

And Mudge let go of the end of scarf he had started to loosen.

"Now, about the school—the one in your head," the Butterfly Lady went on. "Why are you needing a school all of a sudden, with Ned and Serena teaching you everything you want to know? If there's a problem, I was awfully good at recitations. Take Poe—he was one of my favorites."

She jumped up, standing on a slab between two snow-filled urns. Mudge saw her flowered dress splotched against the white background. The Butterfly Lady threw out her arms and said:

> *It was many and many a year ago,*
> *In a kingdom by the sea,*
> *That a maiden there lived whom you may know*
> *By the name of Annabel Lee.*

"It goes on some. Called 'Annabel Lee.' I could teach it to you."

"No," said Mudge. "I mean, maybe sometime, but that's not why I need a school. It's because Aunt Ernestus is coming and she's a stickler, Serena says. Says she'll be upset about Ned teaching me at home—and now Ned's upset and . . ."

"It's a nasty name, Ernestus is," said the Butterfly Lady, climbing down and settling herself once again over "Awaiting the early dawn . . ." "I don't think I shall like her. Where'd you get her, anyway? Thought there wasn't anybody except you and Ned and Serena."

"I guess we've always had her, but nobody talked about her. And just hearing from her has made the house feel funny and Serena and Ned had a fight—and—and—Serena said something about Historic Preservationists—about them wanting to turn it all into a shrine or a monument or . . ." Mudge wrapped his arms around himself and shuddered.

"Oh, them again," said the Butterfly Lady, trying to catch her reflection in the side of a granite obelisk. "They come and they go—ooohing and ahhing and writing down dates and talking about how old everybody is. Poor taste, if you want my opinion. I mean, with some people, age is a decidedly delicate matter. But don't worry. It will blow over—it always does. Now tell me more about this Ernestus."

"Well," said Mudge, settling deeper into the butterfly. "Serena says Ned says she has no imagination and she raised Ned and now she doesn't accept. The way we live here and why—and everything. And now she's coming and we can't stop her. Like the locusts, Ned says."

"Ummm, an apt description. Aunt Ernestus. My, yes, you will need that school in your head. Tell me about it."

"Well," said Mudge, "it was the time I had appendicitis. You know how mostly when we go to the clinic we walk there—me and Serena and Ned—and once we're there we sit in that waiting room, clumped together, like. I've told you."

"Yes," said the Butterfly Lady, leaning forward. "And how you sometimes feel like an island there in the waiting room."

"That's because we never talk to anybody, or save their places when they go for coffee. Ned all the time sitting there reading, and Serena, too. Partly it has to do with Ned liking to keep to himself, and partly Serena says it's because he doesn't like hospitals all that much and when he has to go to one he forces himself to stay there and digs his fingernails into his hands. Like the time I had appendicitis and we went in a taxi and they sent me upstairs to bed and they operated and all . . ."

"Oh, I remember it well," the Butterfly Lady said, smoothing a cabbage rose on her dress. "You weren't here for a good while—and I worried about you. I thought of going over and asking that Frieda, but . . ."

"Anyway," said Mudge, getting up and rubbing his fists up and down the seat of his jeans to get warm. "Anyway, when I woke up afterward there was this nurse and she asked me where I went to school and when I said nowhere she didn't believe me and said of course I did and that everybody went to school and that I mustn't fib and . . ."

"She had an obviously small mind," said the Butterfly Lady. "And then what?"

"There was this kid in the next bed and he was going home and he kept talking about his school, called Woodring, and the things the kids sent him and the teacher and all. He talked about the gym and the playground, the kind of stuff I remember from kindergarten before . . . So when he went home I just sort of took it—the school, I mean—and the next time the nurse asked, or anybody, I just said I went to Woodring school."

"Yes, a small mind, I'd say," said the Butterfly Lady. "The kind who doesn't care what you say as long as you say it.

You'd better hang on to that school—you'll need it with Aunt Ernestus around."

Mudge stamped his feet. "Brrrr, it's cold on that butterfly. I've got to get going."

"Yes, well, you run along now. I guess it wasn't meant for sitting on—the butterfly, I mean. My brother picked that out, though I could never figure why. Do you think it made him think of me? Well, no mind, I've grown quite fond of it. Come back whenever you want and we'll work on our recitations." She stood up and moved over behind the butterfly, leaning with one hand on each wing. Lowering her voice, she spoke distinctly:

> She *was a child and* I *was a child,*
> *In this kingdom by the sea,*
> *But we loved with a love that was more than love—*
> *I and my Annabel Lee—*

And Mudge heard her voice as he trudged toward the gazebo.

Mudge circled once around the gazebo, looking over his shoulder at the pattern his footprints made. He stood on the step and looked down on the city below him, where the black of the street was beginning to wear through. He started down the road in the direction of Jenkins, sliding past standing angels and seated angels and angels holding swords.

"If I go see Jenkins now, I'll just have to go back later,"

thought Mudge, slipping past an angel with a scroll in his hand. "The Captain'll be sure to send me with a message." Mudge scooped the snow off a marker that read "Memento Mori" and shaped it into a snowball, hurling it as hard as he could back toward the gazebo. "Don't see why the Captain just can't go talk to Jenkins," thought Mudge. "You'd think after all that time they were together . . . And he knows Jenkins's gun went off by accident—knows he didn't mean to shoot him. And all the time sending me with messages."

Mudge stopped and stood leaning on a reclining cherub and thought about how he'd like to see all his friends together, perhaps in the gathering room. Then he thought how he couldn't even get them to talk to one another.

"Ahah! There you are. I saw you go up the hill. Thought you might have gone back the way you came," said a voice somewhere in back of Mudge.

"Jenkins? Where are you? What are you doing?"

"Here. Right here." Mudge watched as a wiry string bean of a man backed out from behind a square marker. He was carrying a pine branch and wore a pair of britches and a jacket with buttons down the front. "Needed a stick—to get the snow out of my markings." And Mudge followed Jenkins over to the thin stone marker propped up from the back with several bricks. He watched while Jenkins sat cross-legged in the snow and worked quickly on the letters of his inscription. Soon the words appeared, one after the other.

"Elia Jenkins—whose untimely death was the result of boils for which he was confined to his bed for 102 days and suffered great misery. August 17, 1817."

"There," said Jenkins, jumping up and wiping the stick on the seat of his britches. He went around to the back and rearranged the bricks to make his marker more secure. "That's better."

"I had to do that for the Captain, too," said Mudge, looking up at the sky, which was beginning to lighten around the edges. "Brace up the marker, I mean. Those really old ones, the thin ones, wobble some."

"I'm not surprised. Never could do anything for himself," snorted Jenkins. "Practically had to spit for him. It was always 'Jenkins do this' and 'Jenkins do that.' Had me so rattled most of the time. It's no wonder that gun went off."

Jenkins knelt down and began making an edge of pinecones down one side of the grave. "Wasn't my fault, though. Says so right on the stone. I remember it well from when I used to come, after his time and before mine. Forgotten the exact words now. What's it say, boy?" Jenkins turned the corner and worked his way across the bottom of the grave.

"You know. I tell you every time I come," said Mudge, standing up straight and putting his hand over his heart. "Listen carefully. It says, 'The Captain, who died by the fate of war while he was going through the military manual exercise. He was killed by the discharge of firearms by one of the company which had been loaded without his knowledge or intention. Memento Mori ... 1814.' "

"Humph, must have been some big stone for all that writing. Anyway, you heard what it says." Jenkins stood up from his pinecone border.

"You could go see for yourself," said Mudge. "Besides, I came to tell you something."

"The Captain could come here to see me," said Jenkins, arranging sprigs of holly at the foot of his marker, blocking ". . . great misery. August 17, 1817" from sight. "Thinks he's better than anybody—up there by the pond. Snow could weigh these bushes down, boy. Ought to go through and get it off." He swung his arms from left to right, swirling snow around him. Mudge watched it settle on Jenkins's faded uniform and fringe his eyebrows.

"Well, I guess I'll go. I promised Dorro, and maybe the Captain . . ." Mudge started to back away, carefully avoiding Jenkins's border.

"Thought you had something to tell me, boy," said Jenkins, pausing in mid-swoop.

"Yes, but later. When you're not so busy . . ."

"Yes, I am busy, truth to tell. Been collecting these pine-cones for a long time. Flatten them on one side and they make a better border that way. House-proud, they say, but . . . Go along now, but shake off the bushes as you go. Except his, the Captain's, make him do his own and tell him I said so. Busy, busy, busy," he said, smoothing out Mudge's footprints as he backed away.

Mudge worked his way down the slope away from Jenkins, dodging monuments and markers, stepping over empty flower urns. He crossed the road and turned and ran quickly up the hill.

"Jenkins is doing stuff with pinecones," said Mudge, leaning on the base of the monument and looking up. "And the Butterfly Lady is doing recitations." He stepped back and squinted up at the girl standing next to the statue on the block of marble.

"So what does that make me—third choice?" said Little Dorro, turning so that she stood back-to-back to the stone girl. "Look, I'm as tall as she is, only she's lumpier."

Mudge watched as Dorro inched her way around the front of the statue, running her fingers over the stone face and down onto the ruffled stone dress. "Her nose is sharper," she said. "And the dress looks better on me. What do you think?"

"Oh, I don't think it's supposed to be you exactly," said Mudge, tightening the muffler around his neck. "More the idea of you. A commemoration. Maybe kind of Everygirl."

"Everygirl?" said Dorro, jumping down into the snow. "Everygirl wasn't done in by a milk wagon. Leastways, not at age ten. Oh, it's me all right. But it limits one—stuck there in stone, as it were. No room for growth. So how come I'm last, anyway?"

"Not last—middle. Besides, it's the way my feet took me," said Mudge, looking down at his boots.

"Hmmmph. Comes from not being stuck in stone. Easy enough for you."

"You could, I bet. Move around a bit, I mean. Mind over matter and all that." Mudge held out his hand to her.

"Mind over nothing. What do you know. Bossy thing. And besides, I don't need your help."

"Stop fussing," said Mudge, stamping his foot and drawing his hand back as if Dorro had bitten it. "That's not why I'm here. I have company coming. A relative. Aunt Ernestus . . ."

"So what?" said Dorro as she picked herself up off the ground, brushing herself off. "They do that—kinfolk. Come and stay the longest time. But I guess that's the way it should be, considering how long it takes to get someplace."

"She's driving. Lives about fifty miles from here. She heard we were here and now she's coming."

"A long trip," said Dorro.

"But not like in your day," said Mudge, settling down onto a foot marker. "I've told you that, for pete's sake. Things are quicker now. Anyway, if she stays too long, I don't think Ned can stand it."

"Why not? Doesn't he like her? My papa didn't either, always. Like the kin who came to stay."

"I don't know, but when the letter came, Ned got mad. And he and Serena . . . then he went off to the gathering room and played his guitar. After what happened, you know, I told you about Ned's friend the governor being shot—well, after that, when Serena found them this job and brought us here, they didn't tell Aunt Ernestus. She couldn't accept, Ned says, and I guess they figured she wouldn't approve."

"How could she not approve?" said Dorro. "She didn't even know us."

"Not you she didn't approve of," said Mudge, throwing a snowball down onto the frozen pond and watching it break apart. "Wouldn't approve of us *coming*. She thought Ned should have stayed on being a lawyer—doing what he had been doing."

"But he couldn't have," said Dorro, sending a snowball flying after Mudge's. "Remember when you first came, how it was mostly Serena who did everything—riding on the tractor and edging and trimming. It was a long time before Ned did the stuff he does now."

"Yeah," said Mudge. "But Aunt Ernestus is what Serena calls a practical person. A stickler. And now Serena's getting all upset—saying things like how maybe we shouldn't have come here—and, you know how she gets sometimes, saying I should have more people to play with and . . ."

"You have us."

"Like the time I had appendicitis and she wanted me to ask some kid I met in the hospital to come over. A kid I didn't even know, for pete's sake."

"In a nightshirt?" said Dorro, breaking an icicle off the underside of a marble cross.

"Pajamas," said Mudge. "People wear pajamas now, except he would have worn clothes, I guess, but it was a dumb idea, anyway."

"Mothers are like that some. Mine used to want me to play with Flossie Mae Wilson and she was prissy. But about Aunt Ernestus—I, for one, hope you don't have to spend a lot of time entertaining her. You won't, will you? I mean, I don't guess she'd like reading markers with us, or hunting birds' nests or skipping stones when the pond thaws." Dorro looked at Mudge and held her hand out tentatively to him. "You know what? I think it'll be all right."

"I don't know. We never had a guest before," said Mudge, watching the sky beginning to purple. "Hey, it's getting late and I haven't seen the Captain yet, or the Nickersons. But I can tell you one thing—old Aunt Ernestus won't make me stop coming. Not Ernestus or anybody else."

He looked at Dorro and then beyond to the whiteness and the stillness all around him, and he felt suddenly safe. Safer than he had felt all day. "And you know what else—nothing is going to change."

4

Mudge skirted the upper edges of the pond. The temperature was dropping and the snow was crusted on the top and seemed to catch at his boots with every step.

He stopped by a granite obelisk, tracing the words "Mournfully Memorable" with his fingers, and tried to think what he was going to say to the Captain. Mudge knew that it was better to have his conversation with the Captain tightly wound and ready to go, like a spinning top, before he got there—or risk never getting a word in at all.

He slid out from behind the obelisk and ran a few yards, ducking down behind an angel with flowing robes. He peered out between stone laurel branches and caught his breath.

At first, all Mudge could see of the Captain was the seat of his white britches and the backs of his black leather boots. He was bent at the waist and seemed to be working frantically with his hands. Mudge scuttled to one side so he could see him better.

The Captain was working quickly, shaping one snowball

after another, and adding them to the growing pyramid in front of him. He huffed and puffed, all the while muttering under his breath. Mudge noticed that every few minutes he paused and, without straightening up, twisted one arm around and rubbed the small of his back.

Mudge stepped up onto a slanted granite marker, discovering too late that it was glossed with ice. Suddenly he was flying through the air, with his feet dangling over his face and the bare tree branches spinning around him. He landed in the center of a bush that crackled with the sound of splintering ice and broken branches.

"Halt! Who goes there?" The Captain swung around, his arm raised over his head, his hand clutching a large snowball. "Halt! I say. Halt, or I'll fire."

"Hey, Captain, wait. It's me, Mudge."

"The British are coming. Heading up the bay, they say. Got to defend the fort. Stockpile our ammunition. Cannonballs and . . . Mudge, did you say?" The Captain lowered his arm and kneaded his shoulder with his other hand. He held the snowball behind his back and let it drop quietly to the ground.

"Yes, sir, it's me—Mudge."

"What are you doing down there? With your feet in the air? Not respectful, somehow. Might even say it's desecration of a grave. Might say that, I might, I might."

"Well, sir, it's like this. I slipped—stepped on . . . I mean, covered with ice and . . . It's a bush, anyway. I missed the grave." Mudge struggled to untangle himself, pulling bits of barberry bush out of his red muffler. "Anyway, sir, I came to tell you something." Mudge stood up.

"About the British? Are you a messenger? What's the secret word, my boy? We know about them burning the White House. Scouts have come ahead. Are you a scout? They're heading up the Chesapeake Bay. The British, the British." The Captain seemed to fairly dance around the stack of snowballs, his spindly legs supporting his roly-poly body.

"Come on, my boy. We need ammunition. Need your help. And where's Jenkins? Never here when I need him. 'Jenkins. Oh, Jenkins,'" he called, stepping onto the road. "Have you seen Jenkins?"

Mudge brushed himself off and tried to ignore the trickle of snow down his back between his shoulder blades. "Saw him a while ago, sir. But, sir, about the British—they're not coming. Not now. They came, but it was a long time ago."

"A long time ago, did you say?" The Captain balanced one more snowball on the pile. "And the battle?"

"Battle's over, sir. The British were defeated, and the fort was defended, and all the while it was going on, this Francis Scott Key was out on the British ship and he wrote the words of this song and . . ."

"The battle's over, you say?" The Captain sat down heavily on a marble slab. He took off his worn black hat and scratched his head. "Was I there? I don't recall. Was I brave and . . . Are you sure about the battle?"

"Quite sure, sir. But I'm afraid you weren't . . . I mean—

according to the date on your marker—I'm afraid the accident happened . . . like it says, 'by the discharge of firearms.' "

"That's it. I do remember," said the Captain, putting his head down in his hands. "It was that rogue Jenkins. That scalawag—rapscallion . . . that . . . And to think that I missed the battle." He sighed deeply. "There's something inglorious about it. Ignominious, I'd say."

"Well, sir," said Mudge, sitting on a slab opposite the Captain. "I'm sure if you'd been there you would have been grand. Brave and valiant."

"Oh, do you think so?" said the Captain, looking decidedly brighter. "Would I have been really brave?"

"Brave as a lion. But, sir . . . uh, er . . ."

"Yes, yes, my boy. If you're not a scout, not here about the British . . ." And he paused for just the briefest moment, as if waiting for Mudge to contradict him. He went on. "If you're not a scout and you said you had something to tell me, what is it, my boy?"

"I guess it's not so much—compared to a battle," said Mudge. Then he remembered his tightly wound speech and jumped up, standing in front of the Captain. "It's my Aunt Ernestus. She's coming for a visit and Ned and Serena haven't seen her for ages. She doesn't like us so much, I don't think, except Ned's her brother. Or maybe it's that she likes us *too* much. Or that she likes us but not what we did. It's hard to understand. It's even harder to explain. But anyway, Ned doesn't want her to come, and Serena says . . ." Mudge walked up and down to get his circulation going. "Brrr, it's . . ."

"Brings on my misery," said the Captain, settling in to tell Mudge his symptoms.

But Mudge quickly took hold of the conversation again. "After the assassination, when Ned's friend the governor was killed—you do remember I told you about that, don't you?"

"Certainly, certainly," said the Captain, propping his left leg up and rubbing his knee.

"Afterward, it was Serena who took charge—of getting rid of the apartment and finding us the job here in another city. Serena who packed the boxes and Ned's books. She brought us here, and now Ernestus—"

"That's good. That's good," said the Captain, trying to lean over his round, fat stomach to get another handful of snow. "Relatives coming. That's fine, fine, fine. Tell them I want to know about the British—and how the fort was defended."

And Mudge backed away slowly. Then he turned and ran down the road to the fork, sliding the last few feet. He caught himself on a rosebush and headed up the other road on his way to see the Judge.

The Judge was a listener. He was a ponderer. He was a weigher of evidence and a balancer of facts. But mostly, Mudge knew, the Judge was a listener.

The Judge's place was back away from the road and was marked by a large, stern-faced angel with an open book on his lap. Across the bottom of the monument, chiseled below the angel's robes, were the words: "He Was A Just Judge And An Honest Man, And When He Died He Was Universally Lamented." Even the letters that formed the words were straight up and down and forthright-looking. Enclosing the whole area was a black wrought-iron fence.

Mudge stood outside the fence, feet planted firmly on the ground, arms by his side, and concentrated on waiting for the Judge.

The Judge was tall, well over six feet, with thick white hair that fringed down over the collar of his black alpaca suit. He moved slowly and deliberately, as though every action were carefully measured. Somehow his very deliberateness gave Mudge a comfortable feeling, the way oak trees did, and the warmth of the fire in the gathering-room stove.

"Well, here I am," said the Judge, stepping out from behind an evergreen tree, pushing a small black notebook down into his pocket. "Just stepped over a lot or two, taking a few notes. I've had in mind—listen carefully to this—had in mind compiling a history of Edgemount. A careful cataloging. One can't have too many records, I daresay."

"There already are some," said Mudge, leaning on the fence. "Records, I mean. And there's a plat that tells where everybody is. You, too. On the wall in the gathering room. You could go down and see it."

"Well now, I might have to do that, though I hate to wander off. But it's all for the greater good, lad. History at our fingertips." The Judge was suddenly on the inside of the fence. Hands folded across his chest, he strode back and forth, back and forth. "It ought to be recognized. Hallowed, as it were. Set apart."

Mudge jangled the gate latch sharply. "Is it all right? I mean, can I come in?"

"You can, and you may. Come in, by all means," said the Judge. "Now tell me, lad, there seems to be something on your mind. Some unsettling thing."

"It's just not fair," said Mudge, looking up into the Judge's blue eyes, which were clear as glass. "I mean, Your Honor, sir. It's not fair."

"I daresay, I daresay," continued the Judge, rubbing his hands together. "Things often aren't. Fair. But what particularly?"

"This Aunt Ernestus is coming. Ned's sister. And she's a real stickler—"

"Hmmmm, go on please."

"And Serena says there'll maybe be trouble. About me going to school at home. And Ned's in the gathering room playing his guitar."

"Won't solve anything that way," the Judge said, rubbing his hands together again. They sounded one against the other like crackled pieces of paper. "Now about school. Is it every day and are there regular lessons and books?"

"It's every day, except sometimes we take our Saturdays on Tuesdays and our Sundays on Fridays—or our Saturdays on . . ."

"Er, yes, very good. I understand. What you mean to say is you're flexible. Very good thing, flexibility."

"That's what Ned says, too. And there are books that

Serena orders by mail, and the ones Ned gets at the library, and the ones we have."

"And is there mathematics? And compositions and . . ."

"Yeah, I mean yes, Your Honor. And Latin, too. And astronomy, and mythology, because Ned likes it especially. And poems and . . . The Butterfly Lady said she'd help with recitations, except I already have those. Already know . . ."

"And homework? And examinations?"

"Oh, tons. Of homework, I mean. And maps to draw and . . . and sometimes we're all studying the same thing— Ned and Serena and I—but theirs is harder. And there's music and French . . . and Ned is talking about Greek."

The Judge folded his hands under his chin, tapping his fingers one against the other, back and forth. "Hmmmm, yes, I see. Lessons and maps and mathematics. Latin and French and maybe Greek."

"And mythology, sir. The gods and goddesses and the battles . . . the tales . . . Ned says . . ."

"Yes, well—harumph." He drew himself up straight and tall. "In my considered opinion, this is school, and if Aunt Ernestus questions it, have her come to me."

Mudge started down the road that ran between the vaults. For a minute he stood looking out over Edgemount, but nothing stirred; everything was quiet, except for the grinding city noises on the other side of the wall.

He stopped at the second vault on the right and jumped down into the hole in front—a space where the snow was deeper and the air was sharp and cold. Pressing his face against the bars, he peered into the shadows, sorting out the familiar inscriptions on the slots in front of him. It was a warm, jumbled familiarity filled with "Sarah, cousin of . . ." and "Agnes, beloved aunt of . . ." "Arnold, who was the brother of . . ." "Beloved Father . . . Beloved Mother . . . Beloved Angeline . . ."

"Family coming, you say?" asked a Nickerson that Mudge thought was Sarah.

"Lovely, lovely," chimed in another.

"I'll wager Serena's busy," said a third. "Making calf's-foot jelly. And brandied peaches . . ."

"Grandmother always said . . ."

"Company coming . . ."

And then it seemed to Mudge that all the Nickersons shifted and changed their positions. They all started in again.

"Nothing like a family, I always say," said Angeline.

"Remember the time . . ."

"And Uncle William did . . ."

"It'll be grand . . ."

"Now you, Mudge, you listen to us. Just bring her here to call. Any kin of yours is a friend of ours . . ."

"And don't forget the brandied peaches," said Sarah.

From down the hill came the sound of the funeral bell calling Mudge home before dark, before the cold settled in, hard and still, for the night.

Mudge ran down the hill, watching his breath come in

small white puffs. He left behind the Nickersons and the Judge and the Captain. He left behind Dorro and Jenkins and the Butterfly Lady. But in another way it was as though he took them with him: as though their words were strung together and wound around him, making him warm and terribly safe. He ran faster and faster, fairly flying down the hill.

Inside, the house was warm and smelled of gingerbread. Mudge heard the sound of Ned's guitar, and Serena's, coming from the living room.

He unwound his muffler and shrugged off his coat.

He heard them singing "The Swapping Song," alternating verses.

He kicked off his boots and went through the hall to find them.

5

Mudge sat on the floor of the gathering room with his arms wrapped tightly around his knees and listened to Serena as she read aloud. Ned lay on the rag rug in front of the stove, gently smoking his pipe and watching the smoke puffs spiral upward until they were caught in a draft and pulled sharply sideways.

"Shall we read another?" asked Serena, peering over the top of her glasses. Then, without waiting for an answer, she cleared her throat and read: "Chapter 9. How Diamond Got to the Back of the North Wind."

"Ummm," said Ned. "A good one." And Mudge tightened his arms around his knees and listened to his mother's voice.

At the Back of the North Wind was one of Mudge's favorite books, just as his father had assured him it had long been one of his own favorites. Ned had introduced the book to Mudge and Serena at the same time, and since then they had read it all the way through out loud at least once a year—so that the words had become as familiar as smooth, worn slippers.

Mudge held loosely to the story line and let his thoughts splay out around him. It suddenly occurred to him that if Ned had read the book when he was little, then maybe she—Aunt Ernestus—had read it too. Maybe she had even read it *to* him.

Since that day a week ago when Aunt Ernestus's letter had come, Mudge had been careful not to think about her. He had run races with Dorro and carried messages between Jenkins and the Captain. He had let the Butterfly Lady teach him "The Raven," and then gone to recite it to Frieda. He had taken the Judge to meet the Nickersons and sat cross-legged on the cold damp ground while they told him bits of gossip from all the corners of Edgemount. He had worked with Ned in the gathering room on history and Latin and astronomy. And he knew, from the tight, thin way he held his mouth, that Ned was carefully not thinking of Ernestus either.

While Mudge rushed about, and Ned fixed things that were not quite broken, Serena cleaned the spare room and put sheets on the bed and dug extra blankets out of the cedar chest in the upstairs hall.

And Mudge felt as though something were coming after him: that he couldn't run fast enough: that it was almost upon him.

Serena got to the place in the story where North Wind was sitting on her doorstep and Diamond had to walk through her to get to the land in back. She closed the book with her finger inside, and they sat in silence, listening to the sound of the fire and the ticking of the clock, and thinking about Diamond and the terrible light that was both blue and white.

Serena handed the book across to Ned and he rolled on his side and smoothed the pages flat and read: "Chapter 10 . . ."

And outside a horn blew.

Ned and Serena and Mudge froze, holding themselves immobile while the smoke from Ned's pipe hovered just above them. They waited, listening, hoping that the bleat of the horn was part of the passing traffic out on the avenue.

The horn sounded again, this time insistently. This time clearly coming from the drive under the arch that connected the two parts of the house.

They stood up, and Mudge and Serena watched while Ned lifted the window seat and slipped the book inside, as though it had been planned. And they moved as one toward the door.

Outside, the night was patched with fog; the streetlights cast a yellow glow; and the air that nudged at them was warm and heavy.

The car was black, high and boxy, and seemed to ride in the driveway like a ship at anchor. Leaning forward, over the steering wheel, features blurred by the mist and splintered light, was a woman who Mudge knew must be Aunt Ernestus. And sitting next to her on the seat, eyes melting into the darkness of his sharp and pointed face, was a large black dog.

It all happened in pantomime—Serena stepping up, nodding and beckoning, then back, dropping her arm across Mudge's shoulder and edging him gently forward. Ned standing in the center of the driveway, urging the car along, gesturing and pointing the way, up the drive and sharply to the left to a spot next to Serena's cabbage patch, where no car had ever stood before. Mudge saw his father's face through a shroud of fog. Saw it looking stony white, almost like one of the monuments that lined in back of him into the depths of Edgemount.

The motor stopped and silence settled down around them. Aunt Ernestus sat in the car, staring straight ahead. Ned stood poised on the path, his arms still raised, as if at any moment he might turn and run up the road.

Mudge started around the car—his fingers making track marks in the moisture—muttering under his breath, more to himself than to anyone else: "That's some car . . . Big and . . . and a dog . . . She's finally come."

It was as if in some underlayer of his thoughts he planned to continue going round and round the car—faster and faster—as if, like the tigers in *Little Black Sambo*, he could spin himself out. Round and round; faster and faster. Becoming a mere grease spot on the ground.

"Welcome," said Serena, opening the door and standing back. "Your letter didn't say exactly when you'd be here, so we weren't sure. But come in, come in. We'll have some tea."

Mudge heard his mother's words dwindle as Aunt Ernestus slid out of the car and motioned to the dog, who moved silently to sit beside her.

They stood facing one another, Serena and Aunt Ernestus; stood a few feet away until, without saying anything, they moved together and held one another and stood swaying in the foggy yellow light.

"Ernestus—now just a minute. There was nothing about a dog. Nothing in your letter at all. We can't have a dog here. We just won't." Ned spoke, and it was as though he centered all the force of their separation on the dog sitting at his sister's feet.

"Thanatos isn't an ordinary dog," said Aunt Ernestus, opening the door to the backseat and reaching for her suitcase and her canvas tote bag. "He is well behaved." She dove back into the car and came out holding a large wicker picnic basket, which she added to her pile of belongings.

"Thanatos?" said Ned, coming closer. "Is that your idea of a joke? A pretty poor one—death personified. Fitting, but in poor taste."

"I don't have time for jokes," said Aunt Ernestus, slamming the car door. "Thanatos has been with me five years—and since I just learned your whereabouts a month ago . . . No, he wasn't named in your honor." She flicked her hand, and Mudge watched as the dog followed Aunt Ernestus into the house.

They moved in dumb show: silently: independently: as though each was the only person on an otherwise empty set. And Mudge was the audience.

He sat on the bottom step and watched as Serena put the kettle on and set out mugs and cookies on a plate. He watched Ned, who sorted through a stack of library books on the counter, arranging them first in one pile and then in another.

He shivered and wrapped his arms around himself. Then slowly and deliberately Mudge forced himself to look at Aunt Ernestus. She was tall and straight, with long white braids wound around her head, with a head itself that seemed to sit directly on her shoulders as though she had no neck. Mudge watched as she unpacked the tote bag, taking out a ceramic bowl and filling it with water and putting it alongside the stove for the dog; as she lined a bag of kibble and another bowl on the counter. It seemed to Mudge that Aunt Ernestus had no elbows or wrists or knees or ankles. She looked like the stick people he used to draw, and as if she had a skin of pale pink bubble gum pulled taut across her face.

He moved up another step, back into the shadows, and watched. And when Aunt Ernestus turned away, Mudge suddenly felt that he didn't know what she looked like— would never be able to recognize her again. She turned back into the light and Mudge found himself saying softly, in sudden recognition, "That's her—Aunt Ernestus."

Mudge moved up one more step and propped his elbows on his knees. The energy had gone out of the room. It was as though a row of mechanical toys had stopped and there was no way to start them up again.

Even the dog was still: eyes open, staring without looking at anything.

Mudge looked back at Aunt Ernestus and thought how old she was to be Ned's sister and how she had probably looked old even when Ned was a little boy. He wondered if she had been born with white hair and if she had ever climbed trees or run races. He looked at Ned, still shuffling books, and at Serena, arranging cookies. And back at Ernestus again.

The kettle screamed, releasing them. Ned stepped forward; Serena poured water into the teapot, and Aunt Ernestus swung around, saying, "Come here, Mudge."

Mudge sat for a moment waiting for Serena or Ned to intervene. When nothing happened, he stood up and inched his way down the steps, his hand holding on to the newel post.

"Let me look at you." Aunt Ernestus loomed over him, her arms seeming to go in all directions.

Mudge shrank in upon himself. He rolled his eyes and turned toward Ned. But Ned was looking the other way.

"Come closer," said Aunt Ernestus. And Mudge forced himself to take another step forward.

"Ned is my brother and you are my brother's child and when I found you I had to come. That's all we need to say tonight." And Mudge listened to the words and thought they sounded as if they were made of glass: not real living breathing words that people spoke.

"Oh," said Aunt Ernestus, turning away suddenly. "And I've brought things—things for Ned—his favorites—and for you and Serena too." She rooted in the wicker hamper, pulling out big bowls and small bowls and boxes with waxed paper fringing out from under the lid, and packages tied with string, and handed them to Serena.

"There's black-bean soup and fresh bread and baked custard. Oh, and there are brownies—the kind your father liked as a boy," she said, carefully looking away from Ned. "Here —one tonight." And she broke the string and rummaged in the box and handed a big chocolate square to Mudge.

When the basket was empty, Aunt Ernestus seemed to have nothing more to do. She pushed the hamper back against the wall, then moved it to the other end, then onto the floor by the refrigerator. "It's been a long day," she said, her words stiffening up again. "And if no one minds, I will air the dog and take my tea upstairs."

Mudge held the brownie behind his back, passing it from one hand to the other and feeling his fingers grow moist and chocolaty. "Probably poisoned," he thought. "Or putrid . . . or . . ." And when Aunt Ernestus stepped outside with the dog, Mudge sidled over to the trash can and dropped the brownie in, hearing it thud against the bottom.

"Oh, Mudge," Serena said, in a whisper that filled the room.

Aunt Ernestus and the dog Thanatos came back in. There was a shuffling: a stepping around: a rearrangement until they formed a kind of procession going up the stairs: Serena leading the way with the tea tray; Aunt Ernestus and Thanatos; and, finally, Mudge carrying the suitcase.

Ned stood alone in the kitchen.

Mudge flopped over on his stomach and yanked the blanket out from under him. He could hear Aunt Ernestus in the next room closing the closet door and opening drawers and sliding the suitcase under the bed. Could hear the dog's nails clicking across the floor. It gave the house a crowded feeling.

When he had gone into the bathroom before bed, there had been a strange green toothbrush in the rack and a can of tooth powder and a jar of hand cream on the shelf above the sink. And Mudge had hurried out without brushing his teeth.

He squashed the pillow down over his head, then yanked it off, wiping the sweat out of his eyes. He rolled on one side and then the other, threw his pillow on the floor and picked it up again. He took the clock off the night table and stuffed it under the mattress, the ticking becoming heavy and far away.

He heard Aunt Ernestus's door open; heard the scuff of her slippers and the quiet creak of the floor in the hall, the click of the bathroom door.

Mudge knelt on all fours at the end of his bed, leaning as far as he could off the foot, straining toward the door to the hall. He heard the toilet flush and the funny rat-ta-tat sound the cold spigot made. He heard Aunt Ernestus gargling—as though she were rumbling marbles around in the back of her throat—then spitting into the sink. And his stomach lurched at the sound. He heard, once again, the scuff of her slippers as she padded back across the hall to her room.

Mudge inched his way back into the center of his bed, sitting cross-legged on the bunched-up covers and listening to the creaking of the bed in the next room; the sounds of settling in. His eyes skimmed the familiar shadows in the

room: chairs, a table and a chest of drawers, a cardboard
model of a castle, the shelf over the bed heaped with books
and boxes and a mound that was Oscar.

He stifled a yawn and slapped himself in the face, deter-
mined to stay awake longer than Aunt Ernestus and the
silent dog named Thanatos: now suddenly as close as the
other side of the wall.

6

Mudge woke to the sound of voices that came in under his bedroom door and up the pipes and through the floorboards. They poked and jabbed at him until he was fully awake. His father's voice ran flat and steady under all, while Aunt Ernestus's swooped and pecked, like a bird after seed.

Climbing out of bed, he inched the door open and crept out into the hall, crouching down by the banister and pressing his face against the cool, round spindles. The sound of voices sharpened into words.

"You know, Ernestus, we had to get away. For the good of us all."

"Nonsense! You ran away."

"Good grief—don't start it all again. It's what we did and it's over and . . ."

"You were hiding. You had a duty to the boy and . . ."

Mudge heard the kitchen chair scrape and his father's footsteps across the floor: the firm and final closing of the outside door. He heard Aunt Ernestus's words dipping after him. "It was foolishness. One ought to do what one has to do."

Mudge stayed folded at the top of the stairs. He listened to Aunt Ernestus washing the dishes and sweeping the floor. He heard her go out the door and wondered if she was going after Ned—to talk *at* him some more—and if Ned would continue to walk away from her. Part of him wanted his father to turn around, with his feet wide apart and his hands on his hips, and stare her down. Part of him wanted Ned to keep walking, up past the gazebo, circling down the path between the vaults, looping the pond, and hurrying down around the rose garden—away from Aunt Ernestus and her words.

His thoughts slid away from his father and his aunt, and for a few moments he sat there, testing the uneasy feeling of the house. It was as though someone had given it a good shaking: as if everything had come down topsy-turvy: as if, just possibly, the gathering room might be where his parents' room belonged, with his own room dangling next to the kitchen and the circular staircase going nowhere.

Suddenly Mudge jumped up, pushing at the panic that engulfed him, wanting to be certain of the things around him. He moved first to the door of Serena and Ned's room, holding on to the doorframe and balancing himself as though the floor rocked beneath him. Everything was all right there, and he stood for a moment filling himself with the security of the room: the high bed with steps leading up on either side, the books piled on night tables, and the sunlight through the leaded glass. He moved on to the door of his own room, cataloging in daylight what had been shadows the night before. Mudge looked quickly over his shoulder, then darted forward, reaching up to touch the flattened face of the old monkey. He was back in the doorway before the air had stopped stirring around him.

Next he found himself standing at the door of the spare room, the guest room, looking at the signs of Aunt Ernestus. Already he could sense the layers of her being there: of her sleeping and waking; of the line of her body in the neatly made bed; the slight rearrangement of the rocking chair. He saw her travel clock on the night table next to a stack of Kleenex folded into squares; her purse hanging on the bedpost, and her plain black slippers lined alongside the radiator; her yellowed ivory comb placed precisely on the dresser next to a picture in a frame.

Mudge stood still, wanting to see whose photograph was in the silver frame angled slightly away from him, measuring the distance between himself and the dresser: between himself and the chair. Clenching his fists, he started across the room. Thanatos slithered forward from the other side of the bed. Hackles raised, he stared at Mudge, and his silence, more ominous than a growl, kept Mudge at bay. Then slowly, step by step, Mudge went backward out of the room.

Hurrying into his clothes, Mudge crept past the door of Aunt Ernestus's room. Thanatos's eyes seemed to bore into him long after he was down the steps. He made a peanut-butter and banana sandwich and shoved an apple into his coat pocket as he headed out the door.

Outside, Mudge breathed deeply and listened to the sound

of stirrings. He heard water dripping from the roof, and a general stretching out of branches—a movement deep within the earth that spoke of things that were yet to grow. It was as if last week's snow had been winter's last angry grab. He turned and started up the hill.

Mudge watched Frieda poke at an empty Coke can with the toe of her shoe. She kicked it off to one side, adding it to a pile of cans and papers she had pushed together.

"They got in again last night, huh?" said Mudge, stooping to get an empty popcorn box. "Don't mess with this stuff. I'll get it. Have to tell Ned about them getting in, anyway."

"They left their ladder this time," said Frieda, pointing to a long aluminum ladder slanting from the top of the wall down into the corner of Edgemount. "My goodness, they did have a fine time—fancied themselves spirits, I think —spooking and howling to beat the band. Scared themselves good. Took off up that ladder, hightailed it out of here. And with all that fog, you should have seen them." Laughter seemed to start from the bottom of Frieda's feet and bubble its way upward. She wiped tears off her face and held on to a stone cross to keep from falling. "Oh, oh, oh," she gasped. "It was a sight to behold."

"But don't you care?" asked Mudge. "About the mess they make—but mostly about them getting *in*. It's the only place they do. Ned says it's because the street's highest right here and that makes the wall easier to get to, or something."

"Well, I don't much *like* the mess—but then I don't *mind*

it all that much either. Such interesting things—artifacts, sort of. I've told you, Mudge, Frieda means Peace—not to get riled about these things. And I like a bit of company now and then." Frieda held tight to the cross and gasped with laughter.

Watching Frieda laugh made Mudge forget for a minute the ladder and the people who came over the wall. Suddenly he wanted to laugh, too. Frieda was a small woman, scarcely five feet tall, with a badly twisted back that made her throw her right shoulder forward and tended to make her cave in at the middle. In spite of this, she always seemed to be having a good time. Winter and summer, she wore heavy brown oxfords and lisle stockings and a coat like a sack, with an orange cloche pulled down tight on her head. Once, when Mudge was younger, he had told Frieda that she looked like a bran muffin with a blob of marmalade on top. And Frieda had laughed at that, too.

The inscription at the base of Frieda's cross read: "After Life's Fitful Fever She Sleeps Well. Her Back Was Twisted But Never Her Smile." Sometimes Mudge wondered about that.

"Was it really a fitful fever, Frieda?" he asked.

"Oh, terribly fitful—sometimes, anyway," said Frieda, sitting down in front of the inscription and turning to look at it. "Took myself awfully seriously until I learned . . . and then, well, it's . . . Remember the time you called me a muffin? Oh, ho, ho, ho."

"Seems like it would do for Aunt Ernestus. The part about Life's Fitful Fever—but not the smile. I don't think she knows *how* to smile. Don't think she'll ever learn. Ned says she has no imagination, and now she's here, staying with us. And there's this dog, and he's so quiet. A quiet dog, for pete's sake. And the house seems mixed-up—only it's not really."

"That's one of those things you can't tell about—imagination, I mean," said Frieda, briefly serious.

And Mudge felt suddenly and unreasonably angry: as if Frieda had taken Aunt Ernestus's side against his. "But you don't even know her," he said. "She's a real stickler. Lines things up—neat. She'd never stand for this mess"—waving his hand at the clutter of trash. "And she says she doesn't have time for jokes and . . ."

But Frieda had started to laugh again, quietly at first, then louder and louder.

In spite of the sense of early spring, Mudge felt cold. It was as if all of Edgemount, even this part far up in the corner, the part where kids sneaked in at night and where Frieda laughed and gathered tin cans, was marked by Aunt Ernestus. And he turned solemnly out onto the road.

Mudge ran up the hill and into the gazebo, throwing himself down on the bench, his legs stretched out in front. He ate his sandwich, unsticking the peanut butter from the roof of his mouth, and bit into the apple.

"Is that breakfast or lunch?" called the Butterfly Lady, holding her hand up to keep the sun out of her eyes.

"Either—or both," said Mudge, eating his way around the apple core and feeling suddenly glad to see the Butterfly Lady: as if now things would be all right. "Should have brought more—another sandwich—"

"Oh, that's all right," she answered. "I'm not at all hungry. Not at all."

"That's not exactly what I meant," said Mudge, getting up and starting down to join her. "What I meant was, well, if I'd brought an extra sandwich and maybe some Fig Newtons, I wouldn't have to go back till supper time. *She's* there now. *She* came last night. Aunt Ernestus."

"In all that fog? Poor thing. Not a good night for travel, I'd say."

"And she brought a dog. A funny quiet dog that doesn't *say* anything."

" 'More black than ashbuds,' as the poet Tennyson says."

"I didn't say black," said Mudge, climbing up onto the iron butterfly. "I didn't say any color."

"Oh, but you must have," said the Butterfly Lady, settling back on a marble slab. "It is black, isn't it?"

"Black as night. His name is Thanatos and he seems to have taken over the house—I mean, just by being there. He and Aunt Ernestus."

" 'Let Hercules himself do what he may, The cat will mew and dog will have his day.' That's Shakespeare, you know."

"He's scary and dreadful and he just *stares*," Mudge went on, ignoring the Butterfly Lady, who was leaning on a flower urn.

"Scary, is he? How about, 'Eye of newt, and toe of frog, Wool of bat, and tongue of dog'—that's Shakespeare too."

"I don't *care* about Shakespeare, or Tennyson either. You're just not being serious, and I wanted to tell you. I care about

Aunt Ernestus, and when she's going home, and that dog that just looks at me and . . ."

"I'm sorry if you aren't in the mood for Shakespeare today," said the Butterfly Lady, slightly miffed. "I wanted to do a recitation. Perhaps it's best to stick with Poe, though I don't *think* he's done a dog poem—and I've made a bit of a study of it. But how about 'The Bells'? It has a nice ring to it, if you'll forgive the pun. For myself, I prefer the fourth stanza. Listen carefully." And she stood up and stepped back several paces.

> *Keeping time, time, time,*
> *In a sort of Runic rhyme,*
> *To the throbbing of the bells—*
> *Of the bells, bells, bells—*
> *To the sobbing of the bells.*

Mudge stood up and tossed his apple core into a pile of leaves and started down the hill, away from the Butterfly Lady and her voice, which sounded suddenly like bells. And as he went, he heard her recitation getting fainter and fainter.

Mudge stopped at the bottom of the hill and faced up the road that led to the vaults. From the gullies on either side of the road came the tumble of water: a melting, thawing, rushing sound that displaced the Butterfly Lady's poem and the voices of the Nickersons calling back and forth at the top of the hill.

Mudge had planned on going to the Nickersons, and from

there to Jenkins and the Captain and the Judge and Dorro. Had planned to tell them about Aunt Ernestus coming and about the dog and how they'd taken over the house. But now he wasn't so sure. "With Frieda laughing and the Butterfly Lady saying her dumb poems—bet if Aunt Ernestus were visiting them, they'd care. Bet then they'd . . ."

Mudge planted his feet on the soft edge of the gully and pressed forward, making footprints in the mud. He watched a Y-shaped stick caught in the current and followed it with his eyes until it stuck in a web of leaves.

"No—I'm not going," he said out loud. "Not to the Nickerson's, because they all think relatives are so great—kinfolk this and kinfolk that. Not to anyplace." And he turned and started home, watching the mud dry glistening on his shoes, turning them a shiny blackish-brown.

Back at the house, he ducked through the gathering room and up the circular stairs to Serena and Ned's room and out into the hall.

Aunt Ernestus filled the doorway to his room, standing with her back to Mudge, as though she had been there for a long, long time.

"Is that you, Mudge?" she asked, without turning around. Then, instead of stepping aside, she moved forward into the room.

"Just like the spider and the fly," thought Mudge, inching his way in and standing as far away from Aunt Ernestus as he could.

"Did you have a good day?" she asked absently, turning to examine the room.

"Yeah—yes, ma'am. Okay, I guess."

"I missed you this morning, and then at lunch," she said, stooping to look at the model castle. "Serena says you have friends—people to visit . . ."

"I guess," said Mudge, twisting his hands behind his back to keep from yanking the castle away.

"I hope I'll get to meet them while I'm here," she said, moving a tin soldier from one battlement to another. "There are places I'd like to take you—to the zoo, the museum. Maybe you'd like to bring one or two of them along. That's what I used to do with your father. Would you like that, Mudge?"

"Well, I don't know, I mean . . ."

"We took the grandest trips, picnics and outings, and several times we went to the shore, to the ocean. And we stayed in a hotel and your father swam and collected shells. Did you know that, Mudge?"

And Mudge did know that, without knowing that he knew it. All the way back as far as he could remember, Ned had told Mudge about the ocean: about how they would go there someday. And now the very idea of the shore had been trespassed upon.

Aunt Ernestus moved farther around the room, stopping at the shelves over the bed. "Just like your father's room when he was young. With the books and all. He had books everywhere, and I read to him—to Ned—long after he had learned to read himself, because he liked it that way."

Mudge moved to the other side of the room as though he and Aunt Ernestus were on opposite ends of a teeter-totter and he had to keep the balance.

She reached out and ran her fingers along the edge of the shelf, then suddenly she swung to face him. "Oh, Mudge— there's Oscar. Oscar the monkey. You do remember Oscar, don't you?"

And Mudge remembered: remembered him new and green and yellow: before his face was flat and worn: before his shoes were frayed, with the cardboard poking through. But there was something missing in his remembering.

"I gave you Oscar, Mudge. When you were a little boy and you and your mother and father came to visit me. And you sat on my lap in a rocking chair on the front porch— I was holding you and you were holding Oscar—and we rocked and rocked. Long after it was dark."

Mudge turned to the window.

Behind him he heard Aunt Ernestus continue around the room, as though it were a museum of sorts. When she got to the door, she said, "I meant what I said—about taking you someplace. Anywhere you'd like to go."

After he was sure she had left, Mudge turned and took Oscar off the shelf and hurled him as hard as he could at the closet door.

7

Mudge woke the next day to the sound of voices; and also the day after that and the day after that. But gradually the tenor of the voices changed.

They still came under the bedroom door and up the pipes and through the floorboards, but now they struck a kind of balance: a string of words in Ned's steady voice, followed by a string of words in Aunt Ernestus's slightly higher tones. Then back to Ned again.

One morning, when Aunt Ernestus had been with them for almost a week, Mudge crept out into the hall to take up his listening post by the banister. Suddenly he realized that Aunt Ernestus wasn't talking *at* Ned anymore: that when she said something, he answered her. They talked about when Ned was little and about their mother and father: the grandparents Mudge had never known. They talked about the books they read and about Aunt Ernestus's garden and how Ned used to work along with her when he was small—and how she called him her sidekick, and about the patients she took care of now. They talked about places they had been and places they had never been. And tentatively, hesitantly, they talked about Governor Gordon's assassination; about coming to Edgemount and the kind of life Ned lived there—that little island that was Ned and Serena and Mudge.

And when they talked about this, Mudge could hear his father's answers getting clipped and short. Could sense a restlessness about him. Sometimes he heard the final closing of the door as Ned went off to the gathering room alone. When that happened, Mudge wanted to run down the steps and thumb his nose at Aunt Ernestus and shout, "Ha-ha, Old Aunt Ernestus-pestus. Some things you just can't change, so you may as well go home." But part of him wished that Ned had not gone off, the part of him that hurt when Ned was angry.

After a while Mudge's stomach began to growl. He sniffed the breakfast smells that rose from the kitchen: coffee and sausage and what smelled supiciously like pancakes. He closed his eyes and saw his place set at the side of the table and the bowl of batter he was sure Serena had left next to the stove. He held his breath and listened. The kitchen was quiet. Mudge got up from his niche at the top of the stairs.

Aunt Ernestus sat at the table drinking a cup of coffee. She jumped up when Mudge came into the kitchen. "Oh, Mudge, good morning. I've been waiting for you, to fix you some breakfast. Your mother had things to do and Ned—your father—went off—had things to attend to." She stepped over Thanatos and moved toward the stove. "I'll just heat up the skillet. We had blueberry pancakes, with my own blueberry syrup I brought from home. It won't take a minute."

Mudge ran his tongue around his teeth and tried to erase the warm juicy feeling of popping the blueberries in his mouth. He swallowed hard, choking back the swirl of butter and syrup. "Nope. No, thanks. I'll just have cereal," he said, opening the cupboard and reaching for a bowl.

"What? No pancakes? I never heard of a youngster who didn't like pancakes."

"I'm not hungry, I guess," said Mudge, biting his tongue and shaking some cornflakes into a bowl.

Aunt Ernestus put a glass of orange juice in front of him and took the carton of milk off the table and poured some in a small glass pitcher. "There," she said, putting the pitcher next to the sugar bowl. "That's better. How about eggs—or maybe some sausage. I always see that my patients have a good breakfast. Something to start the day off right. Maybe an omelet?"

"That's okay," said Mudge around his mouthful of cardboard-tasting cereal. "I'm stuffed already." He gave one last lingering look at the skillet—half wishing that Aunt Ernestus would hustle over to the stove, heating and stirring and pouring and flipping. Half hoping she would say, "Don't be silly, Mudge. Of *course* you want some pancakes."

But Aunt Ernestus just added more coffee to her cup and sat down across from him, saying, "Not much breakfast, I'm sure. Not like your father used to eat. He was an eater—Ned was. He was a fine boy who never gave me any trouble. There wasn't much he couldn't do. And, when I'd go for conferences with his teachers, they'd say how well he was doing. And he was good with his hands too—he used to make big beautiful kites and we'd go to the hill on the edge of town and fly them. And there was the guitar—started him as soon as his hands were big enough, and sometimes at night I'd play the piano and Ned would play his guitar."

Mudge listened, with his spoon poised halfway to his mouth. Listened while the Ned he had never known took shape from Aunt Ernestus's words. Suddenly he wanted to hear more. To say, "Tell me about . . ." To ask, "What happened when . . ."

Instead, he helped himself to another bowl of cereal.

"Ned wasn't much on sickness, though." Aunt Ernestus's voice skimmed along. "And when our father was sick and I took care of him, it bothered Ned a lot. Didn't use to want to go in the room—maybe the medicine smell—same way with hospitals. I knew that, and when Ned called to say he was taking Serena to the hospital to have you, I just went right along—met him there and waited with him, got to see you right away."

Mudge pushed the last cornflakes around the bowl and thought about Aunt Ernestus looking at the baby that was himself when he was too small to know he was being looked at.

"I know what you'd like," said Aunt Ernestus, taking a pan down from the top of the refrigerator. "Sticky buns. Made them this morning for tomorrow, but since you didn't have any pancakes—and cereal's a poor excuse for a breakfast." She slid a plate onto the table in front of him.

Mudge's teeth ached with wanting to sink into the caramel coating. His tongue curled around imagined raisins. He looked at the sticky bun on the plate. He thought about Aunt Ernestus talking *at* Ned and talking *to* Ned and he thought of how Ned was beginning to listen to Aunt Ernestus and to talk to her. He thought of how Aunt Ernestus hadn't understood and how she had come to Edgemount now: like the locusts, Ned had said.

Aunt Ernestus went to the sink and turned the water on. Mudge looked at the sticky bun again, and at Thanatos looking at the sticky bun. Suddenly Mudge grabbed it off the plate and held it out, watching the dog gobble it up.

"Maybe it'll poison him and serve her right," thought Mudge, watching Thanatos licking his chops.

Mudge stuck out his tongue at the dog and got up from the table.

He found Serena upstairs in her room going over seed catalogues that were spread out over the floor. She looked up as he came into the room. "Did you have some pancakes, Mudge? Aunt Ernestus's syrup is really . . ."

"Nope. Just cereal," said Mudge, flopping down next to her.

"Hmmm," said Serena, putting a check mark next to a picture of Talisman roses. "Then you really missed something."

"What I've been missing is you. Where do you *go* every morning, Serena, for pete's sake? With Aunt Ernestus talking and talking to Ned, and him all the time backing away and . . ."

"But it's important that they talk, don't you see?" said Serena, turning the pages. "Just the two of them. That's why I've disappeared every morning. There are years for them to catch up on."

"Only you don't know what's happening. You aren't there. What's happening now is that they—Aunt Ernestus and Ned—are talking *to* each other. Sometimes, anyway. It's like she's poking in on stuff. Pushing at him. And sometimes he listens now. And the listening times are getting to be more than the not listening times."

"But, Mudge, don't you see—that's good. That's what we want."

"It's not what I want," said Mudge. "And besides, now she's talking about us being here and asking about school—the way you said she would. And what if Ned stops backing away and listens to that, too. What happens then, for pete's sake?"

He stared down at the picture of the giant marigolds splotched across the front of the seed catalogue.

"Remember, Mudge, how I told you that Edgemount was never meant to be a permanent thing. Maybe, just maybe, it has served its purpose."

Mudge jumped up. "See—you're on her side too—and I'm going out and . . ."

"There aren't any sides," said Serena, tucking her order blank into the catalogue. "Believe me, there aren't any sides at all. But if you're going out, wear your raincoat, it looks like rain."

Mudge ran across the driveway, past Aunt Ernestus's high black car and Serena's cabbage patch. He ran past the rose garden and up the hill, swatting at angels and cherubs and marble lambkins as he went. Circling Dorro's stone marker, he looked up at the stone girl and whistled sharply. He kicked at a clump of dirt, gouging the grass.

"Hey, quit kicking," said Dorro, jumping out from behind a pine tree and flattening the ground with her foot. "And don't whistle at me. I'm not a dog."

"She brought one with her—a dog, I mean," said Mudge, kicking at another clump of ground. "A strange black dog with..."

"I said quit kicking," said Dorro, stamping her foot. "You're supposed to take care of stuff—not make a mess."

"I'm not supposed to take care of anything," said Mudge.

"Well, your mother and father are, then. That's what you're here for."

"We're here because we live here."

"Nobody just *lives* any place. I mean, not without doing stuff. Except maybe us, and it's not quite the same thing. And even we manage to stay busy. Come on—let's *do* something."

"I don't want to," said Mudge, folding his arms across his chest and sitting down on the ground.

"You're just mad because *she's* there," said Dorro, spinning around and making the skirt of her dress stand out.

"Serena says 'she' is the cat."

"That may be," said Dorro, sitting on the ground next to Mudge. "But in this case *she* is Aunt Ernestus. And she makes you cross."

"I wish she'd go home," said Mudge in a small voice.

"Is she awful?" Dorro moved around to face him.

"Well—she's—she eats prunes for breakfast and the pits in the bowl look like eyes staring up at you. And she's always straightening things and she smells like cough drops even when she doesn't have a cold. But the really awful thing is, she just keeps talking to Ned. Long talks, and in the beginning Ned walked away and now he listens and Serena thinks that's good and . . . and I wish she'd go home."

"Yes, but the thing about it is that even if she went home she could always come back. Now that she knows the way, I mean. Come on," said Dorro, standing up. "I'll race you to the fat angel and back."

Mudge shuddered and got up, but by that time Dorro was well out in front, calling over her shoulder, "Come on, slow-poke. Last one there's an Aunt Ernestus."

And Mudge ran.

Mudge and Dorro ran races and climbed a maple tree. They skipped stones across the pond, and when it started to rain, they crawled under a pine tree.

"What's that?" said Mudge, poking at a large wood box with his foot.

"Horseshoes," said Dorro.

"Horseshoes? You don't even have a horse, for pete's sake," said Mudge, pulling the box toward him.

"Not the kind you *wear*—the kind you *play*. I remember at home we had horseshoes—out back under the elm tree—that and croquet," she added wistfully.

"But how did you get them here?"

"They're not mine, silly. They belong to some boy. See, that's his name on the side of the box—Marcus." Dorro took the horseshoes out of the box one by one and lined them on the ground.

"Who? Who's Marcus? What kind of stone does he have? Is he on this side or over by the gazebo? I thought I knew most everybody. I thought . . ."

"He's not one of *us*—he's one of *you*," said Dorro, lining the horseshoes back in the box. "He lives over that way"— and she pointed vaguely in the direction of the wall. "He keeps these here for when he comes to play. He just started coming a week or so ago."

"To play?" screeched Mudge. "What's he coming here for?"

"Why not?"

"It's, well, it's ours—and yours."

"It's pretty here. With trees and flowers. I guess he likes it. Maybe where he lives is crowded, with lots of brothers and sisters."

"Do you *talk* to him?" asked Mudge, jumping up and moving out from under the tree to stand in the rain.

"No. I just watch and listen. Sometimes he talks out loud. To himself. He doesn't know I'm here. But I could if I wanted to—talk to him, I mean."

And Mudge had the same crowded feeling he had had in

the gathering room: as if even the walls of Edgemount couldn't keep him safe any longer.

Mudge trudged home in the rain, taking the long way around, following the road up past the top of the pond and ducking past the Captain's place so he wouldn't see him. He wondered about the boy named Marcus: what he was like and where he lived. When he went past the vaults, he heard the Nickersons calling to him, their voices tumbling one on top of the other, but he didn't stop to answer.

The rain came down harder and Mudge ran for the gazebo, sitting in the center of the floor, away from the driving rain that slanted in from all directions. His hair was plastered to his head and water ran off the end of his nose and dripped on the floor; his corduroy pants were clammy against his legs and his toes squished inside his sneakers.

Mudge looked around for something to do. He wondered where the Butterfly Lady was and thought about dashing home through the rain. He decided there was nothing to hurry home for, anyway.

He heard the sound of approaching footsteps and a muffled voice—and then wasn't sure he had heard them at all. He listened again, trying to suppress the sound of the rain: to hear beyond it.

"Mudge—oh, Mudge." Mudge heard the voice just as Aunt Ernestus appeared in the doorway of the gazebo. She was swathed in an olive-green poncho and had a plastic rain bonnet tied under her chin. She stood, still holding her umbrella, and let the rain drip off her and make splash patterns on the gazebo floor.

"Oh, good. I've found you. It came on to rain and I wasn't sure . . . didn't think you had your raincoat . . . thought I'd bring it along." And she held the yellow slicker out to Mudge.

The gazebo seemed damp and sodden and suddenly awash. Mudge pushed himself back, the seat of his pants grating against the floor. He wanted to yell at Aunt Ernestus: to ask her who she thought she was and that nobody came after him and what did she think he was—a baby or something— and does she think he's going to melt in a little bit of rain and why can't she just leave him alone, for pete's sake. Mudge wanted to say all these things: but he looked at Aunt Ernestus, still holding the umbrella, with her face all shiny and slicked with rain, and he stood up and reached for the slicker.

Mudge started down the hill after Aunt Ernestus, his feet slogging in the puddles, his slicker open and the hood deliberately pushed back, the water running down his neck.

Aunt Ernestus waited for him at the bend, standing next to a marble fawn, her umbrella tilted as though she were trying to protect the animal's head.

"Do you know what this reminds me of, Mudge?" She went on without waiting for an answer. "A time when Ned was younger. It started to snow during the day and I gathered up your father's galoshes and his heavy scarf and took them along to school for him." Aunt Ernestus stopped suddenly, as if the ending of the story still came as a surprise to her. "And he didn't want them: Ned didn't: he was angry and said that I'd embarrassed him in front of his friends. And I carried those boots on back home."

Mudge trailed behind Aunt Ernestus, watching her shoulders hunched slightly forward, her poncho dipping down in back to reach her boots. Part of him wanted to cheer the boy Ned for telling Aunt Ernestus off.

But suddenly and inexplicably a deep-down part of Mudge was sorry for Aunt Ernestus trudging home in the snow carrying the offending boots.

And he hated himself for feeling sorry.

8

Mudge was angry all during lunch.

He was angry with the rain for raining and with Aunt Ernestus for bringing his slicker, and with himself for wearing it. He was angry with Ned for making Aunt Ernestus carry the boots back home that snowy day many years ago, and for inviting Aunt Ernestus for lessons in the gathering room after lunch today; and with Aunt Ernestus for saying she would come. He was angry with Dorro for playing with Marcus's horseshoes and with Marcus for leaving them there in the first place and with Serena for talking on and on about seeds and bulbs and hybrids and perennials—and for fixing grilled cheese instead of tuna fish for lunch.

It was a grumpy, irascible, sullen anger that made him grind his feet onto the rungs of his chair and turn down Serena's rice pudding even though it was his favorite dessert.

It was a consuming, gobbling-up kind of anger that made Mudge feel he had gotten out of bed on the wrong side—and broken a mirror and walked under a ladder.

And it festered and grew, and ballooned around him.

After lunch, Aunt Ernestus came to lessons in the gathering room. She tapped on the door and opened it and stuck her head around the side, saying, "I hope I'm not too early."

"Come in, Ernestus. Sit down anywhere. We're just finishing our Latin for today, and then we'll . . ."

Aunt Ernestus sat on the mourner's bench on the far side of the room, signaling for Thanatos to lie on the floor at her feet.

And Mudge felt a shifting of the room around him: as if the men and women who still seemed to inhabit the gathering room had moved sharply to one side.

He chewed the end of his pencil and smudged his paper and stared at the Latin verb in front of him. To invade: *invado, invadere, invasi, invasum.*

He turned his chair so that he couldn't see Aunt Ernestus and tried to pretend she wasn't there.

invado	*I invade*
invadis	*you invade*
invadit	*he, she or it invades*

He wrote slower and slower, shaping the words carefully, dragging them out. Hoping that Aunt Ernestus would get tired and leave.

invadimus	*we invade*
invaditis	*you invade*
invadunt	*they invade*

Mudge heard her moving in back of him and he clenched his shoulders and held them tight. He heard her go by the bookcase and Serena's desk and stop to study the plat hanging on the wall. He looked down at what he had written and saw the words "Aunt Ernestus invades—he, she or it invades—*invadit*"—and couldn't remember writing them.

Turning the page of his notebook quickly, he saw the same words indented on the clean white page: Aunt Ernestus invades—he, she or it invades—*invadit*. He turned another and another page until all traces of what he had written had disappeared.

Aunt Ernestus seemed to be memorizing everything: the wood stove, Serena and Ned's guitars, the dictionary on a stand. She stood by the back window, her fingers tracing the panes, and slowly, carefully, as if some outer force were driving her, she raised the window seat and took out the copy of *At the Back of the North Wind*.

Mudge stopped, his pencil frozen in mid-air. And Ned went to stand beside his sister.

Aunt Ernestus opened the book, turning the pages carefully, as if they might break. Mudge saw her smile a funny, distant smile and point to something on a page. He saw Ned reach across and turn a few pages and show her something else. Together they stood, looking at the book, Ned and Aunt Ernestus, sharing a conversation without words that was so loud that the noise clattered and caromed against Mudge.

Aunt Ernestus closed the book and stood holding it against her chest, her arms folded across it. Ned turned, as if remembering Mudge for the first time. "Well, Mudge," he said in a hearty, un-Ned voice, "how about telling your aunt what you are doing in Latin."

"No," said Mudge.

"Mudge, we have a guest."

"We don't have guests—not in the gathering room. At least, we never did before . . . the way it used to be . . ." Mudge pushed at Ned with his angry words.

"Mudge." Ned leaned on the table, his face close to Mudge's. "I am asking you to conjugate your Latin verbs for your aunt. She is our guest."

"I won't," said Mudge.

"You will—and you shall," his father said.

"To invade," said Mudge, jumping up. "*Invado, invadere, invasi, invasum*. Third person singular: AUNT ERNESTUS INVADES: HE, SHE, OR IT INVADES: INVADIT: AUNT ERNESTUS INVADES," Mudge yelled.

The room was silent. Even the clock seemed to have stopped.

And Ned turned from Mudge and said in a voice that was as cold as stone, "You will go to your room and stay until you are told you can leave it."

Mudge sat and stared at the back of his bedroom door. It looked blank and hostile and had a closed-upon-him feeling: different from when he closed the door himself—when he chose to be alone.

But Ned had closed the door just as surely as if he reached

all the way from the gathering room and up the steps through his and Serena's room and out into the hall. As if Ned-fingers had been waiting there to slam the door behind him while a Ned-voice repeated from downstairs, "Go to your room, go to your room, go to your room."

Mudge had come the long way: out the door of the gathering room and across the drive; around back and through the kitchen door. He had gone past Serena, who was kneading bread, and stumped his way up the steps without saying anything: without answering Serena, who called after him, asking what was wrong and where he was going.

And now he stared at the back side of the door and watched the light outside turn thin and lemony, and the day begin to slip away.

Mudge had never been sent to his room before. He never really remembered being punished: always before, if something was wrong, he and Serena and Ned would talk it out.

"It's not fair," said Mudge out loud, looking around the suddenly alien room. "It's just not fair—and it's all her fault. Pushing, pushing. All the time pushing. And she does invade and then I just *had* to say that and Ned got mad and . . . Should have stayed where she belonged. Things were okay until she came, would still be okay . . ."

He got up and walked up and down his room: quietly at first, and then with great thumping footsteps that seemed to echo around him. Every once in a while, Mudge would stop and listen. Then he would start to pace again, lifting his foot slowly and heavily. One foot and then the other.

"It's a wonder it doesn't have a ball and chain on it," he

mumbled. "A wonder they don't put me on a chain gang." And as he walked from the window to the door and back again, Mudge seemed to see himself in a black-and-white prison uniform. "A wonder they don't throw me in a dungeon or something, and feed me bread and water." And he suddenly saw himself huddled next to his straw pallet in a dingy cell—gnawing on a crust of bread.

Mudge heard Aunt Ernestus come up the stairs and go into her room and then go out again and down the steps. From the kitchen he heard cooking sounds and smelled a spaghetti smell. But still no one came. Once he thought he heard someone calling him and he yanked his door open—but there was nothing except the sound of water running in the kitchen sink, the opening and closing of the refrigerator, and the voices of Ned and Serena and Aunt Ernestus talking to one another.

"Boy," thought Mudge, kneeling at the window and looking out over Edgemount. "Bet the Butterfly Lady would *do* something. She wouldn't stand for this—or Frieda, either. I ought to go see the Judge, get him to . . ."

The door opened behind him and Serena came into the room, flipping on the light.

"I thought we could talk a bit before dinner, Mudge," she said.

And Mudge wondered fleetingly if that meant *he* was going to get dinner: wasn't really going to live on bread and water. But still he stood facing the window.

Serena came up behind him and put her hands on his shoulders. "We have to talk, Mudge. Your father didn't want to punish you. He hates to do it. But you must admit you asked for it—saying what you did."

And Mudge felt a sudden welling up of tears inside his throat and he shrugged away from Serena and moved to the other side of the room.

Serena waited, letting the silence pile up between them, and finally Mudge said, "It's her fault. Ned said he didn't want her to come, that people have a right to be left alone."

"Those are Ned's words, Mudge. Old words—and they were angry words," said Serena, sitting on the bed. "I'm glad you're loyal to your father—but sometimes we have to let people fight their own fights, because otherwise when they resolve it we are left wielding a sword when the battle's over."

"Is the battle over?" asked Mudge, still standing, but turning to face Serena.

"No. Not over. But maybe a truce. The thing you have to remember is that Aunt Ernestus loves Ned—perhaps she has had to learn to temper that love—but she *is* learning. And she loves you, too, and I'd hate to see you deprive either one of them of that."

"Me?" said Mudge quickly. "Me again. Why is it always me? I didn't tell her to come, and ever since she's been here, I'm all the time getting in trouble and punished and yelled at and stuff—"

"Oh, Mudge," said Serena, putting her hand in front of her mouth. "You may be exaggerating just the tiniest bit. It's a funny thing, you know—but the more people we admit into our lives, the more vulnerable we become. And that's not necessarily a bad thing. I don't know—but maybe Ned and I have deprived you of something by our way of life."

"No," said Mudge. "I like it."

"Maybe you should do more things—go out and . . . Remember the movies I told you about at the library—it would be a place to meet friends."

"But I have friends right here, and they don't make any trouble. They don't . . ."

"But we're missing the point," said Serena, standing up and going toward the door. "You were rude to Aunt Ernestus and you have to do something about it."

"You mean, I've got to apologize? To say I'm sorry? I can't . . . I . . ."

"Well, that too. But I think you can do more. For Aunt Ernestus and for Ned—for all of us."

"More what?" asked Mudge, sitting down abruptly. "You mean apologize and more?"

"How about this," said Serena. "Aunt Ernestus has been wanting to take you out—someplace—maybe the zoo or the Science Center or the museum. You could go with her, let her do something for you. To make up for what you did to her."

"No—no. I won't. Me and Aunt Ernestus—yipes, Serena, I'm not going. Not going clomping all over town with her. And besides, I like it here. Don't want to go. I'll do anything else. Apologize ten times, a million times. For pete's sake."

"Then take Aunt Ernestus out with you."

And Mudge felt the floor tilt beneath him. "With me where? I don't go . . ."

"To Edgemount. You can take her to all your favorite places. Show her the things you like. After all, she hasn't really had a proper tour since she's been here."

"Oh, Serena," groaned Mudge. "Do I have to?"

"You have to. Tell her you're sorry for what you said and then tell her you'd like to take her around tomorrow."

"Tomorrow? Why not later—another day."

"Tomorrow," said Serena, opening the door. "Come along. You can do it now. Think how much more you'll enjoy your dinner once you've said you're sorry."

And Mudge followed Serena out of the room and down the steps.

9

Aunt Ernestus told Mudge it took a "big" person to apologize —but Mudge didn't feel very big as he trudged along behind her the following morning.

It seemed to Mudge that lately he had been coming "after" people: following Serena down steps and Ned and Aunt Ernestus up paths and along walks. He wanted to break loose: to run free. He wanted to race through Edgemount as he had always done: sailing over fences and skirting monuments; snaking in and out of tombstones and leapfrogging over low sprawling bushes.

He shook his arms and swung them from the shoulders as if to rid himself of some invisible shackle. He jerked his legs to loosen an unseen hobble, and kicked at a flat gray stone and watched it skim the path. He wanted to unencumber himself. To move unburdened and unfettered. And Aunt Ernestus was definitely an encumbrance.

"And Thanatos, too, for pete's sake," thought Mudge, kicking the stone again and trying to catch up. "Big deal. I'm supposed to be showing Aunt Ernestus around and there she is, leading the way. And the dog, too. There I am, following a dumb old dog."

Just then, Aunt Ernestus stopped where two paths met. "Which way from here, Mudge? You're in charge."

And Mudge stood looking around him as though newly arrived in a strange land. He squinted and held his hand up to his eyes. It was a day of such strong white light that everything seemed bleached, like a photograph that had been too long in the sun. The sky was blanched and dipped down on all sides to touch the ashen trees, the waxen shrubs. The monuments and markers were pearly and appeared to recede into the colorless background. The road lay like a ribbon that had been drained of its color, and even Aunt Ernestus, waiting expectantly for Mudge, had a doughy cast to her face. Only Thanatos stood out in contrast: sharp and black.

"Which way, Mudge?" prodded Aunt Ernestus.

And Mudge shook his head, struggling against a tiredness that overtook him. "What difference does it make?" he thought. "Serena said to take Aunt Ernestus and I'm taking Aunt Ernestus. She didn't say I had to *like* it—that it had to be fun, for pete's sake. And she said 'Do it for Ned'—and what does Ned care? Going off to clean around the vaults and acting like it's just any old day. No big deal."

He shrugged his shoulders and turned to the left. "This way, I guess. It doesn't matter—doesn't make any difference. It's just a place. Nothing special." And the words pinched inside Mudge.

"But your mother tells me you really like it here, that you have favorite places to go." Aunt Ernestus huffed a little on the incline. "And it's nice of you to take me around. I want to see everything—go everywhere."

"Yeah, well, we can start up here, I guess," said Mudge, wondering what Aunt Ernestus would think of Dorro: what Dorro would think of Aunt Ernestus. He noticed the long, stalky grass by the side of the road and the leaves clogging the gullies.

"I really wanted to take you out somewhere," said Aunt Ernestus, starting forward again as though she had put herself in gear. "We could have had lunch, just the two of us, and gone somewhere. But this way Thanatos gets to come along." She reached down and touched the dog's head. "And there'll be plenty of time for the other—plenty of places to go."

And Mudge felt himself tightening like a fist.

They stood in front of the monument with the statue of the stone girl on top, and Mudge noticed that her nose was chipped, that there were dark water stains in the marble folds of her dress, and that the base was pockmarked along the edges. He stood for a moment, expecting Dorro to jump out at them, to come darting around the corner. But instead there was a heavy silence.

"Well," said Mudge, pulling at a weed at the base of the statue. "This is just a—just a place. A place I come sometimes. I don't know—it's . . ."

"Very interesting," said Aunt Ernestus, walking slowly around the statue and pausing to read the inscription. "And so young—such a young age to depart. Wonder what happened—what the cause was."

"Milk wagon got her," said Mudge, then quickly clamped his teeth down onto his tongue.

"What was that?" Aunt Ernestus called. "There was a lot of that, children dying young, before we had our modern drugs—antibiotics and all."

Mudge had a sense of someone watching him: of someone laughing. He tugged at his collar and looked over his shoulder. "Hey, Dorro, come on," he whispered, pulling at the branches of a pine tree and peering inside. "Hey, come on— I brought her and . . ."

"Did you lose something, Mudge?" said Aunt Ernestus. "Maybe Thanatos can help. Finds my glasses when I misplace them. Finds them every time."

And Mudge had a sudden picture of Thanatos scenting out Dorro, racing up and down hills. "No, it's okay," he said, dropping the branch of the evergreen tree and watching it sweep the ground. "Come on, let's go. There's nothing here."

"This is the pond," said Mudge, hurrying Aunt Ernestus along. "Sometimes it freezes in winter and you can slide on it—or skate. And in summer it's . . . Well, it doesn't look too good now and the grass needs cutting, I guess, and the bushes, too." Mudge looked at the shrubs gawking out in all directions; at the grass growing in uneven tufts. Even the water looked muddy and still.

"Some of the graves up here are old, kind of," said Mudge,

calling back over his shoulder, urging Aunt Ernestus along. He stepped off the path toward the Captain's place, wondering what he would be up to today: whether he would accuse Aunt Ernestus of being a British spy.

"Oh my, yes," said Aunt Ernestus, stooping down to make out the inscription on the Captain's stone. "1814—an antiquity, I'd say. You can tell it's old, the way the letters are worn thin. Hard to make out the name—" And she traced the Captain's name with her fingers.

"Come on over here," said Mudge, wanting Aunt Ernestus away from the stillness and the terrible quiet.

They skimmed by the Judge's place, circling the wrought-iron fence, while Mudge looked over his shoulder and listened for the Judge's voice. Somewhere a pigeon cooed, making the silence that much louder.

Mudge waited while Aunt Ernestus admired a marble cherub leaning on a cross. He pulled at vines circling the cherub's outstretched arms and said, "It's kind of a mess—overgrown, sort of." He wondered at the weeds that suddenly seemed to be creeping over all of Edgemount.

Mudge led Aunt Ernestus down the road between the vaults. "Ned's here," he said. "Cleaning out the entrances to the vaults, where all the leaves and junk collect over the winter." He strained his ears, listening for the voices of the Nickersons. "Here I've brought them a real live relative—and where are they?" Mudge thought. "All that talk of calf's-foot jelly." He listened again and heard only the scrape of Ned's rake against the stone.

"Oh, there you are," said Ned, hoisting himself up out of the place where he was working. "Place's a bit of a mess right now—trying to make some headway. With the winter and all." Mudge wished that his father wouldn't make excuses for Edgemount; wouldn't apologize in front of Aunt Ernestus. And suddenly he remembered how he had done the same thing and the remembering had a bitter taste. "I can help later on," he said. "As soon as I—when we're finished, I mean," said Mudge, kicking at a clump of weeds.

"We're having a lovely tour," said Aunt Ernestus. "So much to see." Mudge looked at her quickly, but she was bending over, reading a footstone.

He took her to Frieda's place, strangely neat and quiet; and then on to Jenkins's. Aunt Ernestus moved slowly around Jenkins's grave, careful not to step on the border of stones and pinecones. "How lovely," she said. "And so well cared for. And another old stone." She leaned forward, reading the inscription out loud: "'Elia Jenkins . . . untimely death . . . result of boils . . . 1817.' Boils, poor man," she said, straightening up. "And look at the date—that would be near the time of the War of 1812, same as the one back there a ways. Wouldn't it be funny if they knew each other—back then, I mean. Did you ever think of that, Mudge?"

And Mudge made his face go smooth and flat and headed on past the gazebo toward the Butterfly Lady, pulling Aunt Ernestus along as if by invisible strings.

The Butterfly Lady stood on a marble slab with her back toward them, her arms outspread.

> *Gaily bedight,*
> *A gallant knight,*
> *In sunshine and in shadow,*
> *Had journeyed long,*
> *Singing a song,*
> *In search of Eldorado ...*

she said in a singsong voice. As soon as the verse was finished, she began again:

> *Gaily bedight,*
> *A gallant knight ...*

"What a handsome butterfly," said Aunt Ernestus, swooping down and walking around it. Mudge thought he heard the Butterfly Lady pause briefly before she hurried on:

> *But he grew old—*
> *This knight so bold—*
> *And o'er his heart a shadow*
> *Fell, as he found*
> *No spot of ground*
> *That looked like Eldorado ...*

"Got to go," said Mudge, glaring at the Butterfly Lady's back. "Time to go home for lunch," he said, raising his voice to a shout, trying to drown out the voice that went relentlessly on:

And, as his strength
Failed him at length,
He met a pilgrim shadow—
"Shadow," said he,
"Where can it be—
This land of Eldorado?"

After lunch, Mudge pushed the wheelbarrow from one side of the road to the other, making a zigzag pattern as he trundled his way up the hill on his way to the vaults.

"A wasted morning," he said to himself over the rumble of the wheels. "Dumb old nobody being there—and dumb old Aunt Ernestus saying all during lunch how it was 'lovely, just lovely,' and dumb old Thanatos. Dumb. Dumb. Dumb."

He dropped the wheelbarrow with a clatter and called to the Nickersons, who were chittering among themselves. "Hey, where were you guys, anyway?"

"Is that you, Mudge?" called a Nickerson named Sarah. "Come to help your father?"

"Worked awfully hard this morning," chirped Angeline.

"Yeah, well, he's coming back this afternoon—but before he does, I want to know where everybody was—brought Aunt Ernestus along and ..."

"Oh, we were busy, Mudge. Busy, busy, busy," sang out Uncle William Nickerson.

"Lots to do, and lots to do," chimed a cousin distantly.

Mudge kicked the wheelbarrow as hard as he could and limped on down to Frieda's place.

"Well, you're back, I see," he said, rubbing his foot against the back of his leg. "I came here—brought my Aunt Ernestus to visit you, and . . ." He watched while Frieda kicked a Coke can across the grass and hurried, laughing, after it. "Hey, cut that out," called Mudge. "You're supposed to be a grown-up—old, sort of—and there you are, playing kick the can. And where'd you get that Coke can, anyway? It wasn't here this morning." But Frieda disappeared behind a mulberry bush, leaving only a tracing of laughter behind her.

He found Jenkins polishing the pinecones with the edge of his coat. "Ah, boy—it's good to see you. Wouldn't by any chance have a handkerchief, would you—to polish with. Oh, I thought not. Just wondered, though." And Jenkins bent closer to his work, wedging the corner of cloth into the crevices of a large pinecone.

"Where were you, Jenkins?" Mudge fairly shouted. "I came here and you were gone. Some friend . . . some . . ."

"Had to go on a search, boy," said Jenkins, looking somewhat affronted. "My border needs replacing—have to be on the lookout . . ."

Mudge heard the Butterfly Lady before he saw her. Heard the rise and fall of her voice as she said:

> *"Over the Mountains*
> *Of the Moon,*
> *Down the Valley of the Shadow,*
> *Ride, boldly ride,"*
> *The shade replied,—*
> *"If you seek for Eldorado!"*

"I've got it at last," she said, stepping off the slab and turning to face Mudge. "That's called 'Eldorado' and it's by Poe— Edgar Allan Poe. I believe I've mentioned him to you."

"We were here—this morning—Aunt Ernestus and I, and you didn't even speak, just kept right on like a broken record."

"I don't believe I saw you," said the Butterfly Lady. "I was practicing my recitation. Good for the mind, you know." And she threw back her head and began again,

> *Gaily bedight,*
> *A gallant knight,*
> *In sunshine and in shadow . . .*

Mudge went back by the vaults, but Ned hadn't come yet. The wheelbarrow lay where he had left it, toppled into a gully, and the rakes were leaning against a tree trunk. He ran along the road toward the Captain's place, but somehow the thought of listening to the Captain tired him and he veered over to see the Judge.

"Hi, Your Honor, sir," called Mudge, approaching the

gate. "I was here before—brought my Aunt Ernestus because Serena said I had to—it was a punishment, actually—a sentence, sort of."

"A sentence, you say. Did the punishment fit the crime?" the Judge asked, looking up.

"Well, sort of, I guess. But you weren't here. No one was—anyplace, I mean."

"Well, yes—yes—harumph. Went down to see that plat you were telling me about. Looked through the window of the gathering room . . . a splendid room, by the way. A splendid house—old, and ought to be preserved . . . ought to . . ."

And Mudge backed quickly away.

"I thought you'd be back," said Dorro, swinging her legs from her perch at the feet of the stone girl. "Though how you had the nerve after what you said—'Just a place . . . just a place . . . nothing here,' " she minced.

"Well, there wasn't anything here," shouted Mudge. "You weren't here . . . and nobody else. Not the Captain or Jenkins or the Judge, for pete's sake. Not Frieda or the Nickersons—and the Butterfly Lady just kept on saying her dumb old poems . . . and even now, when I went back, everybody's doing something. I mean, even Frieda's kicking a can—at her age. And I brought Aunt Ernestus up here this morning. Gave her a tour, for pete's sake."

"Bet someone made you," said Dorro.

"Well, yeah, but . . ."

"Well, the truth is," said Dorro, jumping down and putting her hands on her hips. "If you want the truth, which you probably don't, but I'll tell you anyway, because that's the way I am—I mean, I tell people things."

"What things?" said Mudge.

"Things like—we were here. Or we could have been, except you weren't especially nice to Aunt Ernestus—what with her seeming like an okay person and all. And that dog's okay, too—like one we had at home when I . . . before . . . I mean, you didn't seem to *care* about her—and isn't it the caring that matters, after all?"

And Mudge felt outside of things. He went slowly back to the vaults and began to work, raking the wet, clammy leaves and scooping them up and putting them into the wheelbarrow.

10

"So you see, I have to get home," said Aunt Ernestus, standing at the door of Mudge's room. She waved the telegram, as if for emphasis, but the yellow piece of paper flopped limply in her hand.

"Had to send a telegram to tell me I was wanted, needed, at home," said Aunt Ernestus, edging farther into the room. "My friend Annie—they're bringing her mother home from the hospital, a stroke you know—and I said I'd be available to help. Oh, I do wish you had a phone. Telegrams are so imperative, and besides . . ."

"No," said Mudge, pushing himself up against the headboard of the bed. "We've never had a phone. Ned says they intrude—they . . ."

"But now that we've . . . now that I've come . . . seen you and Ned and Serena—it's a way of keeping in touch."

Mudge watched Aunt Ernestus looking around the room and thought for the first time about keeping in touch. Ever since Aunt Ernestus had come, Mudge had waited for her to go home: had waited for the time when it would be just him and Ned and Serena: when the gathering room would be given back to the people who claimed it and his friends at Edgemount were free to be just his friends. And now Aunt Ernestus was talking about keeping in touch—and maybe coming back—and even the possibility of Mudge coming to visit her.

". . . thought I'd come for a final visit, if I could find a place to sit," said Aunt Ernestus, going in circles in the middle of the floor.

"Oh," said Mudge, staring for a moment at the clutter of books and jeans and dirty socks on the chair. "Oh, yeah," he said, jumping up and shoving everything on the floor.

"That's better," said Aunt Ernestus. "I promised Annie before I came that I'd help her out with her old mother— told her just to get in touch. The telegram came this afternoon while you were helping your father. Oh, I almost forgot . . ." She rooted in her apron pocket, pulling out a gingerbread boy with a pink icing coat. "I made these this afternoon." And she put the gingerbread boy on the table next to the bed.

Suddenly it seemed that all the conversation had been drained out of the room: as if someone had lifted the plug and let the words and the remembering swoosh away. Mudge picked at his fingernail and stared at the water spot over his window. He listened to a mockingbird in the elm tree outside and strained for the sounds of traffic from the avenue that ran along the far side of the house: outside the wall. He counted the books on the top shelf of his bookcase and the knotholes on the underside of the shelf over his bed. He rummaged in the back of his mind for something to say.

"Ned liked gingerbread boys when he was young," said Aunt Ernestus, as though she had speared the thought as it went drifting by.

"Oh—yeah, well," said Mudge.

"It was a nice trip this morning that you took me on," said Aunt Ernestus, trying again. "A fine trip."

"It was a rotten trip," thought Mudge, chewing a nail. "Dumb. And nobody was there—and then you got me in trouble with my friends. You and Thanatos." Mudge put his finger in the book he had been reading, squeezing the pages down around it until the finger felt fat and numb.

"I'm glad I came, Mudge. Here, I mean. To Edgemount," said Aunt Ernestus.

And Mudge felt as though a ball were flying toward him: that he had to catch it.

"Yeah—me too," he said, as the words almost went skimming by.

"Probably not," said Aunt Ernestus shortly. "Young people need friends—children to play with. I'm sorry I didn't meet any of your friends. Hope they didn't stay away because I was here . . ." Her words dwindled off.

And suddenly it seemed to Mudge to be terribly important that Aunt Ernestus be glad she had come: that she think *he* was glad. He scrabbled around for words and thought about Dorro saying Aunt Ernestus was an okay person. He let his fingers slide out of his book, losing his place.

"I have this friend and she'd really like to meet you sometime. Says you sound okay. And besides, Aunt Ernestus," said Mudge, all in a rush, "I'm glad you came. Really glad." And he crossed his fingers behind his back and wished he meant the words he had said.

"Oh, Mudge, that's lovely—lovely," said Aunt Ernestus, wiping at her eyes. "I won't see you in the morning—we'll get an early start, Thanatos and I—but, well, Mudge, I'll come back. Especially now—I'll come back to you and Ned and Serena."

Aunt Ernestus stood up and for an awful moment Mudge thought she was going to come closer: maybe even kiss him: breathe on him with her cough-drop breath.

"And something else," she said, her arms making chopping motions in the air. "If there's ever anything—if you need me for anything, I mean—I'll come."

"Oh, no," said Mudge. "There's nothing. I mean . . ."

"There was a time," said Aunt Ernestus, launching into a story, "when your father was young, that I told Ned this same thing. And of course Ned never was one to admit he needed anything. He was going off to stay with our great-aunt—when our father was dying—so we devised a system —a joke, if you like—that if a dragon came, he was to call me. Funny, but I always saw myself as warding off dragons— and believe me, Mudge, we all have our own particular dragons."

And she was gone, leaving Mudge alone to think about Ned and dragons and Aunt Ernestus. He reached over and picked the raisin eyes out of the gingerbread boy and ate them. He held the cookie and licked off the pink icing coat.

Mudge lay back on the bed and propped his right foot on his left knee. He wiggled his toes and tried to move them one at a time. He thought about Ned—and saw him as a kind of puzzle he was taking apart bit by bit. Instead of piecing him together, he was unpiecing him: knowing Ned from the inside out, because of Aunt Ernestus.

He ate the arm of the gingerbread boy, and then the other arm, and catalogued the things he now understood about Ned: why he loved reading, and especially reading aloud, and working in the garden. Mudge ate one leg and then the other, and the body too, chewing slowly and deliberately and poking his tongue around the inside of his mouth to get all the spicy ginger taste. He examined bits of his father, setting him against a background he had never known before: Ned learning the guitar and flying kites and being afraid to go in the room of his own sick father: Ned and Aunt Ernestus, who was a carer—and Ned struggling against being cared for too much: and finally learning to care for a friend —and that friend being killed. Ned who sang about the Lonesome Valley and who even now was downstairs laughing and talking to his sister and his wife.

"Yipes—I ate it," said Mudge, jumping up and holding the gingerbread boy's head at arms' length. He ran to look at himself in the mirror, checking his color and the whites of his eyes, sticking out his tongue and peering down his throat.

"Looks okay," he said, turning away from the mirror. He

popped the gingerbread boy's head into his mouth and climbed in bed. He turned out the light and went to sleep.

The next morning, the feeling of Aunt Ernestus being gone pervaded the house. It filled the room and was caught in the dust motes suspended in sunlight and in the voice of the mockingbird outside in the elm tree.

Mudge lay still for a moment, listening, and looking at the ceiling. Then he jumped out of bed and ran out into the hall. Aunt Ernestus's bedroom door was open and the room was filled with spaces. There was a space on the floor where her slippers had been, and on the bedpost where her purse no longer hung. There was a space on the dresser instead of the ivory comb and brush, and a suitcase space under the bed. The travel clock was missing from the night table.

Mudge tiptoed into the bathroom. He ran his finger along the glass shelf over the sink, exploring the emptiness left by Aunt Ernestus's jars and tubes and bottles. He took a piece of toilet paper and spit on it, wiping away the barely perceptible film of tooth powder, then drying it until the shelf squeaked back at him.

From downstairs came the sound of a guitar and Mudge stood still and listened to his father singing:

> *Do you ken John Peel with his coat so gay,*
> *Do you ken John Peel at the break of day ...*
> *Do you ken John Peel when he's far, far away,*
> *With his hounds and his horns in the morning ...*

And Mudge was downstairs in the kitchen before Ned got to the second verse.

"She's gone. She's gone. Like she said—and I could tell. I could smell it." Mudge ran and looked out the back door. "No more prunes. No more smelly menthol cough drops. No more Thanatos. No more Aunt Ernestus."

He paused and looked on the floor where the dog's water bowl had been, and on the counter for the kibble and the extra bowl.

And Mudge wondered why he didn't feel as good as he thought he would.

"It was a good visit," said Serena. Mudge held his breath, remembering Serena saying, before Aunt Ernestus even came, "Maybe it will be all right"—and Ned's sudden surge of anger.

"Yes," said Ned, playing the refrain of "John Peel," "it was a good visit."

"And now it's over," said Mudge, spreading jam on a piece of toast.

"I don't think things are ever really over, Mudge," said Serena. "They usually seem to continue on—or melt into other things. This was a case of melting in, I'd say."

"But she's gone," said Mudge, looking from Ned to Serena and back to Ned again, and thinking of the sudden emptiness of the room upstairs. "Really gone. And the dog, too."

"She's gone," said Ned. "But it was a comfortable kind of going. And I think that now Ernestus can do what she couldn't do years ago—accept the way we live here. And for our part . . ."

"Our part?" said Mudge, pushing his plate across the table. "Our part's fine . . ."

"And for our part," Ned went on as though Mudge had not spoken, "maybe some of what Ernestus said made sense. Maybe it is time to look at things again." Ned strummed his guitar, singing under his breath as though he were in the room alone.

"Well, it was okay and all, I guess. Aunt Ernestus being here—but I'm glad she's gone. Glad it's just the three of us again," said Mudge. "Glad we can be the way we were."

"Speaking of the three of us," said Ned, putting his guitar on the table, "we're going out—you and Serena and I—going out, and you're not even dressed."

"Going out where?" asked Mudge.

"To the library. I want to find some books on . . ."

"But I don't want to go. I have to see Dorro and . . ."

"Oh, do come, Mudge," said Serena, shaking seed into the bird feeder. "There's a secondhand bookstore I've been telling Ned about and he's promised to stop there today, and then, afterward—it was supposed to be a surprise, but I'll tell you now—we thought we'd have lunch out. There's a Mc-Donald's near the library, and we thought you'd like to eat there."

"What for?" asked Mudge, putting the bread in the bread box and the butter and jam in the refrigerator. "We never eat out—why do we want to eat lunch out?"

"But, Mudge, it will be fun. Most boys would . . ."

"Most boys? Most boys? That's Aunt Ernestus talk. You're only doing it because she said to. We never went out before—

it was always okay here and you always said it didn't matter about most people. We were ourselves—that's what you said." And Mudge looked from his father to his mother as though they were impostors wearing parents' masks.

"Don't be ridiculous, Mudge," said Ned, getting up from the table. "It's hardly a matter of principle. It's just a trip out, to the library and to lunch. It's supposed to be fun."

"Well, it won't be fun and I don't want to go."

"Suit yourself," said Ned. And Mudge sat back down and breathed a heavy sigh.

"But your mother and I are going, anyway," Ned went on, looking over Mudge's head to Serena.

"You're going, anyway? Just the two of you?" asked Mudge, looking hard at Ned.

"Yes," said Ned. Then, "Yes, we are," in a firmer voice.

"But what about me?"

"We'd love to have you come," said Serena. "But if you don't want to, if you have things to do, well, there's plenty here for your lunch."

"But you never do that—go somewhere both of you at once," said Mudge.

"We're going," said Ned, as though he had to hold tight to a string that might suddenly be yanked away.

"You're old enough, and we won't be gone too long," Serena spoke into the cupboard as she reached for her coat.

After they had gone, Mudge felt as though he were without an anchor. He could never remember a time when Ned and Serena had gone off somewhere together, leaving him behind. There had been plenty of times when he had been alone in the house—and one or the other of them had been up on the grounds; plenty of times when he had wandered the paths and roads of Edgemount, sometimes for a whole day at a time, but either Ned or Serena was always at home.

Suddenly he felt giddy with weightlessness. As if at any moment he might go bobbling through the room, grazing the ceiling and the doorframes, nudging his way out the back door and bouncing along from tree to bush to granite monument, and maybe even clearing the walls. He pulled himself back, pushing his bare feet down against the floor, and let the silence mold itself around him.

"She's gone," he shouted. "Aunt Ernestus-pestus is gone." And Mudge laughed out loud: a booming, bouncing, ricocheting laugh that careened around the room like a metal ball sprung suddenly loose inside a pinball machine. He stopped, letting the laughter race on without him, remembering that Serena and Ned were gone too and he was alone in all of Edgemount. And that aloneness crowded him.

Mudge ran up the stairs and hurried into his clothes and ran back down again as if something were after him. He went out the door and up the path, kicking a stone, then running to catch up and kicking it again.

As he neared the path to the vaults, he heard a shout—a spate of jumbled words that said "LOOKOUTBELOW I'MCOMING-DOWN." The words were caught in the wind and the hurtling, tearing body that collided solidly with Mudge.

"Hey—why'nt you look where you're going?" said the dark-haired boy from where he lay sprawled on the grass.

"Me? Me? I was just walking along minding my own business and you come shouting out of nowhere," said Mudge, picking gravel bits off his hands.

"Did not. I yelled 'LOOK—OUT—BELOW—I'M—COMING—DOWN.' Who's Aunt Ernestus, anyway?"

"How did you know about Aunt Ernestus?" asked Mudge, standing up and brushing at the seat of his jeans.

"That's how I knew you were coming—why I shouted. Heard you coming along singing some dumb song about Aunt Ernestus-pestus has gone away." The boy stood up and switched to a sudden, sharp falsetto as he sang again, " 'Aunt Ernestus-pestus has gone away—doo-da, doo-da. Aunt Ernestus-pestus . . .' Oh, crimeny . . . THE KITE." And he looked suddenly at the string still held loosely in his hand. "If you made me ruin that kite, I'll . . . I'll . . ."

"What kite? I didn't see any kite—just you coming down that hill on top of me, then splat," said Mudge, glad to be away from the subject of Aunt Ernestus. Away from the song he didn't know he'd sung.

"It's red with a yellow tail and my Pop gave it to me for my birthday and if it's smashed I'll smash you."

"Why don't you just follow the string?" said Mudge. "Here, I'll help you."

And together the two boys started working their way back up the hill, snaking their way over angels and railings and crosses and bushes.

"There," said Mudge, pointing to the top of a stubby evergreen tree. It's stuck . . . don't . . ."

But the dark-haired boy was already standing on tiptoe to dislodge the kite. He held it in his hands and turned it carefully all around, the red tissue paper making a fluttering sound.

"Looks okay to me—what do you think?" And he thrust the kite at Mudge. "I'm Marcus, by the way. And it's lucky for you that kite's okay."

"Marcus? You're Marcus? Then they're your horseshoes in the box under the tree near Dor . . . Under the tree up by the pond."

"You found my horseshoes? How'd you know they were mine?"

Mudge shrugged and made a great study of turning the kite this way and that. "Hey, it's light, isn't it?" He said the first thing he could think of, to keep from telling Marcus about Dorro finding the horseshoes and spreading them on the ground underneath the pine tree.

"Light? That has to be one of the world's all-time dumb remarks. It's heavy, how you going to get it to fly? Tell me that?"

"I just meant—well, you know, it's big and you know how sometimes you pick up something big and it sort of flies up and gets away because it's not heavy, I mean. Yeah, it looks okay to me."

"Good. Then we can fly it," said Marcus, rewinding the string. "What's your name, anyway? You live around here?"

"Mudge. And yes, down there by the gate. The gatehouse."

"Hey, neat," said Marcus, stopping for a minute to look at Mudge. "That's an okay house. Come on."

"You shouldn't fly it here," said Mudge, following him up the hill.

"Says who?"

"Says nobody. It just makes sense, 'cause there's too much stuff for it to catch on."

Marcus reached the top of the hill and turned around. "You ever try to fly a kite on a flat old city street with cars and trucks and about ten million kids and old ladies with shopping carts all the time saying, 'Watch where you're going, sonny.' We may as well—it'll get smashed when the kids at home get hold of it. Come on." Marcus turned and started to run, calling back over his shoulder, "I'll get it started, then you come along and catch onto the string. We'll fly it together."

Mudge saw him throw the kite into the wind; saw it catch and pull upward. And Mudge ran after Marcus, catching hold of the string, stumbling along behind him. He felt the glorious, soaring-into-the-sky tug at the end of the string. He felt as though he had been flying a kite forever: as though, in part, he was Ned a long time ago on the hill outside of town. They veered back and forth, dodging markers and rosebushes, stepping over gullies and tumbling into a heap.

They rewound the string and started over—again and again—with Marcus in the lead and Mudge running to keep up, the yellow kite tail fluttering high above their heads.

"Wow, I got to go," said Marcus, rewinding the string and examining the kite after their last trip down. "Got to help my father in the store. See you tomorrow, okay?"

And Mudge watched him go down the drive and under the archway, holding the kite carefully against the gusting wind.

That night Ned took *At the Back of the North Wind* out of the window seat in the gathering room and started to read aloud where they had left off.

Mudge tried to concentrate on the story: on how Diamond described the country in back of the North Wind.

But instead, superimposed over all, once again Mudge saw his father and Aunt Ernestus standing on either side of the book.

He listened to his father's voice and watched the shadows on the wall—and briefly it seemed as though Aunt Ernestus had not left.

11

"I told you I'd be back," said Marcus when Mudge opened the door on Sunday morning.

"Oh, well, yeah, hi," said Mudge, his words tumbling one on top of the other. "But I have to eat. Serena's fixing it now."

"That's okay, I'll wait." Marcus stood firmly in the doorway, peering over Mudge's shoulder. "What's she fixing—your mother?"

"Pancakes, because it's Sunday. Most days we just get what we want ourselves."

"I like pancakes," said Marcus, shifting first onto one foot and then the other.

"Me, too."

"The kite's okay except there isn't any wind, so I left it home. How come you call her Serena if she's your mother?" Marcus inched slightly forward.

"I don't know. I just always have I guess. And Ned is Ned."

"Boy—my pop'd let me have it if I called my mom Serena."

"Is your mother named Serena, too?"

"No, dummy. Her name is Rose, but he'd let me have it if I called her Rose. Smells like those pancakes are pretty much done," said Marcus, sniffing loudly.

"Yeah, I guess." Mudge moved back a bit to keep Marcus from stepping on him and wondered why, if he could tell breakfast was almost ready, he didn't leave.

Serena came up behind Mudge and pulled the door open wide. "Did I hear you talking to someone, Mudge? Hello— who are you?"

"My name is Marcus," said the boy, taking his hands out of his pockets and standing up straight. "I'm a friend of his and yesterday I brought my kite and we flew it together and today maybe we'll use my horseshoes and . . ."

"And you'll come in and have some breakfast with us, won't you? We're having pancakes," said Serena, stepping back and motioning for Marcus to come inside.

"Hey, this is neat." Marcus looked around the kitchen. "How about that part that goes over the driveway—is that a real room?"

"It certainly is, and after breakfast Mudge will show you around—this part of the house and the gathering room as well, where the mourners used to wait a long time ago. Call your father, Mudge, while I set a place for Marcus. Oh, Ned, here you are . . . Come and meet our guest."

Guest: our Guest: my Guest. Mudge examined the idea of a guest from all directions. He thought of Aunt Ernestus, who had turned the spare room into a guest room—and of Marcus sitting across from him, eating pancakes. Part of him wanted to pull at the corners of his mouth to keep from grinning. Another part of him felt uncertain about showing Marcus through the house: about sharing the gathering room and the circular stairway and the room over the arch.

"I'm not too hungry," said Marcus, pouring syrup over his stack of pancakes. "I've already had breakfast at my house— eggs and bacon—because it's Sunday," he said, nodding at Mudge. "Then I came over here looking for you. To invite you over. My mom said to, 'cause it's my little brother's birthday and there'll be cake and stuff and all the family'll be there. But not till later. We have time to do stuff first. I was going to go get out the horseshoes, but I saw all those people with wreaths and all and . . ."

"A birthday party? That sounds like fun, doesn't it, Mudge," said Serena.

"All what people?" asked Mudge.

"The ones who were there. Way up by the pond, and they kept checking names off and waiting for more people to come. If nobody wants that last pancake, I'll just . . ." And he reached out with his fork.

"Oh, I forgot," said Ned, settling back and opening a book. "They're the group from the General Society of the War of 1812. They wrote that they were coming—to honor the veterans. They bring wreaths and somebody says a few words. A little ceremony."

"But that's the Captain," said Mudge, jumping up. "And

Jenkins. *They're* veterans of the War of 1812. You mean, there are people at the Captain's?"

"Captain who?" said Marcus.

"But it's all right," said Ned. "I knew they were coming."

"But he might not like it," said Mudge. "The Captain, I mean. All those people. And Jenkins—the way he keeps everything neat and all . . . everybody tramping around."

"All right, Mudge," said Serena, putting her finger up to her mouth. "Not now. Who would like some more? It won't take a minute and . . ."

"Jenkins who?" said Marcus.

"Come on. I got to go. To get up there. To see if there's anything I can do." Mudge headed for the door, calling over his shoulder to Marcus. "Come *on,* I said."

"But, Mudge, the party. Marcus asked you to his house. Are you going?"

"Yeah," said Marcus. "Birthdays are big at our house— even if he is a little kid. And it's close by," he said, turning to Serena. "Up the avenue to Silver Street and two blocks over. My pop runs a grocery store and we live upstairs."

"Yeah, well, maybe," said Mudge. "I mean, thanks for asking me and all. But first we have to get up there. Come on."

"Hey, wait up," said Marcus. "Thanks for the pancakes. Hey! . . . You crazy or something?" he called, running along behind Mudge out the door: as, the day before, Mudge had run along behind him when they played out the kite string.

The boys arrived just as the ceremony was about to begin.

"We'll start here and move on to the others after a while," said the little man with the tightly furled umbrella clamped under his arm, who seemed to be in charge. "Now, let me see—are we all here, all set?" And he scribbled something on his list.

"See, I told you," said Marcus, jabbing Mudge in the ribs. "Told you there were people. C'mon, let's go before somebody makes a speech."

"Shhh, we've got to stay," said Mudge, inching forward. "It's for the Captain."

"What's so special about this guy, anyway?" asked Marcus, pointing to the Captain's stone, which was lightly fuzzed with lichen.

"Well, he's old. Been here a long time, I mean. And he was from the War of 1812. And it worried him a lot that the British were coming and he really cared about defending Fort McHenry, only he didn't, because he died beforehand. By mistake, because Jenkins's gun went off accidentally and Jenkins was his aide and he felt really rotten and so did the Captain and now . . ." Mudge stopped short at the look on Marcus's face.

"Yikes. You talk like they were real. Like you knew them or something."

And Mudge felt as though he were balancing on a teeter-totter: as if one step in either direction would send him tilting wildly off into space. For the smallest moment he wanted to go on: to tell Marcus everything he knew about Jenkins and the Captain; about Frieda and the Judge and the Butterfly Lady. He wanted to grab hold of Marcus and take him to meet Dorro: to have him join in while they climbed trees and skipped stones and searched for birds' nests. It was the same sort of feeling that made him, in some inside part of himself, want to go to Marcus's house: to the birthday party. He wanted to share with Marcus—but there was a stiffness, a newness, about this sharing that made Mudge clamp his teeth down on his tongue.

He looked at Marcus again. At the blunted edges of his face, as he said, "How'd you know all that stuff anyway? How do you?"

"From Ned. I know it from Ned, and he gets it from records, I guess. Records and stuff that are kept in the gathering room." Mudge said the words all in a rush, then he turned his back to Marcus and moved closer to the group just as the little man with the umbrella cleared his throat and began to speak.

And in that particular area of Edgemount, by the upper edge of the pond, along the curve of the hill where the wild strawberries grew in spring, Mudge heard the conversations that stretched around him: heard them in bits and pieces. And he was part of all of them.

"We are gathered here today . . . fitting and proper . . . recognition that is their due . . ." the man with the umbrella intoned.

"Look, my boy—see who's behind that obelisk," the Captain whispered out of the corner of his mouth. "It's Jenkins—thinks I don't see him there. Could have waited his turn. They'll get to him. Hush now, don't want to miss this."

"Crimeny—it's almost like being in church," said Marcus, pushing at Mudge from behind. "Let's *go*."

"Valiant soldier . . . faithful service . . . bravery and . . ."

"A nice touch," muttered the Captain. "Especially the part about gallantry. You hear that, boy? Hear that, Jenkins?"

"Next thing you know, they'll sing something. Come *on*—let's go." Marcus kicked at the ground and sent a stone skittering across the grass. "We'll go to my house."

"Here today . . . Honor to the veterans of the Great War of 1812 and now . . ."

"Psssst," called the Captain. "The wreath—he won't forget the wreath, will he?"

"I'm going," said Marcus out loud. "There'll be birthday cake and the grandmothers and aunts and uncles and my pop'll kill me if I'm late."

"A fitting commemoration . . . an auspicious occasion . . ." The umbrella man's voice seemed to gather force as he concluded his speech.

"That was a fine speech. Hope they do as well by you, Jenkins. Well, almost as well."

"I said I'm going," said Marcus, working his way backward onto the road.

And the people seemed to break out of their group, forming themselves into smaller groups. They drifted around

Mudge, nodding and smiling and speaking to him and to each other and to no one in particular.

"A fine ceremony . . ."

"I do enjoy these get-togethers . . ."

"A lovely day . . ."

"Such interesting markers. Dating back . . ."

"A real history lesson . . ."

"Beautifully maintained . . ."

"All the lots filled . . . now just a matter of preserving what is here . . ."

"Ought to be set aside . . ."

"Oh, my dear, but don't you know? The State Historic Preservationists have been working on this for years. To have it made a Historic Site . . . especially the gatehouse. Unique unto itself . . ."

"From what I hear, they have almost raised enough money. Should be only a matter of time . . ."

And they gathered their bundles and purses and walking sticks and followed the man with the umbrella along the road to Jenkins's place.

"Should be only a matter of time . . . a matter of time . . . a matter of time . . ." The words filled the air around Mudge like a kind of pulse—beating and beating. "A matter of time . . ." until they gradually faded away.

And Mudge was left standing alone in the place where the crowd had been, with the grass flattened down and the wreath of red carnations tilting crazily against the Captain's stone.

From somewhere in that welter of words he remembered

Marcus saying, "I'm going. I said I'm going." And he felt suddenly empty.

Mudge looked around for Marcus, self-consciously at first, in case he was hiding from him. He looked under the ever-green tree and in the branches of the maple and in back of the obelisk, where Jenkins had listened to the ceremony. He looked on the pathways and across the road and at the edges of the pond. He started to run, stopping by the half-opened box of horseshoes and through the newer part of Edgemount and past the rose garden. He clamored up onto a high marble cross and leaned forward, his arms resting on the wall, looking into the street and searching for Marcus.

Then he started to run; zigzagging through the markers and monuments and over the garden, down the main drive-way, and under the arch. Suddenly he was in the middle of Edgemount Avenue.

The emptiness of the Sunday streets came down around him. The few cars and taxis going by seemed to menace him, to shout and roar at him more than the everyday traffic he usually saw from across the wall. Mudge stood in the mid-dle of the street as if his feet were glued to the faded yellow line. He looked back at the house with its drawn window shades, which gave it the appearance of a face without ex-pression. He swayed backward and forward—unable to move.

He heard a roar and saw a pack of motorcycles looming toward him. The one on the end swerved at him, looping around in the middle of the street and circling him. "Hey, kid, get out of the street. What're you trying to do?"

Mudge jumped back. He heard a screech of brakes, the blast of a car horn. He darted forward, pushing his way through the weight of the exhaust fumes that hung over the street. He clung to a lamppost on the other side of the street and closed his eyes.

He started to walk, stepping over broken glass and wads of chewing gum flattened onto the sidewalk. A yellow cat came close and rubbed against his legs, and as Mudge leaned down to pat her, she arched her back and walked away.

He continued on up the street, past the Elite Tavern, with the sign creaking overhead and the throb of music coming from the open door. He inched his way around a group of men laughing and talking on the sidewalk, and past the laundromat, where the air was steamy hot.

Mudge wanted to go back. He wanted to run across Edgemount Avenue and scramble up the side of the wall, pulling himself along by the tangle of vines, and drop over onto the other side, landing in the rose garden. But some part deep inside of him wouldn't go back: some part wanted to find Marcus.

He heard the siren before he saw the engines. The sound whined and swelled and filled the air around him. A dog sitting on the stoop threw back its head and howled. The sidewalk shook beneath Mudge's feet as the fire trucks lumbered past. Mudge looked for the dog and found him cowering in a vestibule, and for a moment Mudge wanted to crouch there with him, hands over his ears.

He ran forward to the corner, turning into Silver Street, stopping suddenly. He looked at the mailbox and the fire hydrant with red paint smeared across the orange. He saw a scraggly tree growing out of hard brown dirt. He looked up the street, straining his eyes to see if he could find Marcus.

Mudge felt as though his feet wouldn't move: as though he couldn't go any farther—backward or forward: as though he would have to stand there forever with all of the life on Silver Street going on around him. Slowly, he worked his way forward, past the narrow houses lined one next to the other. He tried to remember where Marcus had said he lived. Two blocks down—or maybe three, or four. Across the street, this side, cater-cornered. Mudge didn't even know the name of Marcus's father's store.

Suddenly, stores seemed to spring up all around him: on corners and in between: food stores and drugstores and shoemaker shops. Candy stores and bars and meat markets. Stores that laughed and jeered at him: talking stores, and those that just stared silently. All around him, things seemed to grow larger and larger and push down on Mudge. The palms of his hands were wet and his stomach hurt. He looked around wildly and then he turned and started to run. He ran away from the stores and the houses and the scraggly trees; away from Marcus and his brothers and sisters and the birthday party that didn't matter any more. He ran back to Edgemount—up the drive and under the arch—and stood leaning against the inside of the wall, feeling sad and lonely and happy and safe: all at the same time.

12

"We could do this later," said Mudge, making squiggles down the side of his paper and twisting his feet around the rung of his chair.

"No," said his father. "We'll finish math and history and then you can take a break."

"But, Ned, I've got something to do. Someplace to go. I promise I'll . . ."

"Say there, Mudge, do you think if you were in regular school you could just . . ."

"But I'm not in regular school," said Mudge. "I thought it was good to be flexible."

"Flexible is one thing—casual is something else. Seems to me you've had a few too many days off lately. Maybe Ernestus was right when she said . . ."

And Mudge gulped and pulled his paper toward him and began to write.

He finished the math problems and checked them and

corrected the mistakes. He answered his father's questions about the history chapter and listened while he talked about the life of Harriet Tubman and her part in the Underground Railroad. It seemed to Mudge that Ned's voice went on and on: that it would go on forever. It seemed that the chair he was sitting on grew harder and harder: that the hands of the clock no longer moved: that time itself had stopped.

Mudge thought of the day before: of running across Edgemount Avenue and up to Silver Street: of running home again. He tightened his arms across his chest and pulled his knees up, clenching his insides. He had not told Ned and Serena about what had happened. When they asked, he told them carefully that he had not gone to the party; that it was a baby party, for pete's sake; that he would go to Marcus's another time. He was somehow afraid that this new Serena and Ned had wanted him to go—to eat ice cream and cake and play games with Marcus's brothers and sisters. He shuddered and was glad he was safe in the gathering room. He wondered if he would ever see Marcus again.

Mudge slid down in his chair and stared at a point slightly to the left of Ned's head. STOPTALKINGSTOPTALKINGSTOPTALK-INGSTOPTALKING. He sent thought waves toward him. STOP-TALKINGSTOPTALKINGSTOPTALKING . . .

". . . for tomorrow. Okay, Mudge?" Ned's words grabbed at him, sounding very much like the end of something.

"What? Huh?"

"I seem to have something less than your undivided attention. I'll bet you were so busy wanting me to stop talking

131

that you didn't hear a word I was saying," said Ned, breaking into a grin.

"Well, yeah, but you see I've . . ." Mudge felt his face beginning to burn.

"Okay. Run along. But, as I was saying, some time before tomorrow, check those library books I brought home the other day and see what you can find out about Harriet Tubman on your own."

And Mudge wondered, as he hurried out the door, what there could possibly be left to find out that Ned hadn't already mentioned.

Mudge stood in the middle of the drive, looking up at Edgemount. Everything was sharp: the monuments looked scrubbed and the grass was bright and green and neatly trimmed. Birds sang and the air was clear: nothing looked faded and scraggly as it had when he had taken Aunt Ernestus around. Nothing looked worn and grimy as the world of Silver Street had. Mudge took a deep breath that reached almost to his feet and started up the hill. He was worried about Jenkins and the Captain: about whether they had felt invaded yesterday; had minded the ceremonies and the people tramping back and forth: had missed their usual Sunday-stretching-into-eternity quiet.

Marcus lay on a marble slab with a flower urn at either end, with his hands folded behind his head. "Well—look who it is," he called. "Thought you'd still be up there, poking after that guy with the umbrella and listening to funny speeches."

"Oh, hi," said Mudge, ducking his head and hurrying on.

"Wait," said Marcus.

"They were for the Captain," said Mudge, walking faster.

"Hey," said Marcus, sitting up. "I'm talking to you, and you'd better stop."

And Mudge stopped.

"Boy, is my mom mad at you. And my pop too. And my brothers and sisters and my aunts and uncles and even the grandmothers. You better just hope they never get hold . . . never catch you . . ."

Mudge backed slowly down the hill. "Well, you could have waited," he said softly, kicking at a clump of weeds. Then louder: "You could have waited."

"Why should I?" asked Marcus, standing up and moving toward Mudge.

"Because you invited me and . . ."

"And you were hanging around dumb guys with flowers —crimeny, and they were making speeches and, besides, I told you I was going . . ."

"And I was coming," said Mudge. "Honest . . ."

"Yeah, and so's Christmas. That's what my pop always says—'so's Christmas,'" shouted Marcus, beginning to dance in a circle around Mudge. "And anyway, you could have come on your own—could have, if you wanted. It's just up there, couple of blocks."

"You should've waited," yelled Mudge, sensing the emptiness of his words. "You should've."

"Yeah, well, maybe you're a spook. A ghost living in a graveyard and never going any place . . ."

"Do too," said Mudge.

"Do not."

"Do too—go plenty of places. Go to—to the—just the other day, Serena and Ned went to a place called McDonald's and I could have gone too but I didn't want to. I could go any place I wanted."

"A place called McDonald's," jeered Marcus, moving faster and faster around Mudge. "*Big deal*. Everybody goes to McDonald's. I could go there every day if I wanted. Every day in the whole year. So there."

"And besides—I like it here," said Mudge, turning quick small circles inside Marcus's larger ones. "And anyway—it's better than Silver Street with all that traffic and broken glass and . . ."

"Bet you never saw Silver Street. Bet you never saw anything."

Mudge turned away from Marcus, still hearing the shuffle of his feet on the ground behind him.

"Hey—what do you mean, turning your back. I'm telling you stuff—talking to you." And Mudge felt a sudden thump in the middle of his back that propelled him forward.

He swung in an instant, without waiting or thinking, and his fist caught Marcus on the top of the arm.

Marcus lunged, catching Mudge around the knees and toppling him to the ground, and they rolled together in a heap. Mudge felt himself being ground into the dirt, felt stones and sticks pressing into his back—then suddenly he was on top, pummeling Marcus into the ground; and he was down again—watching trees and clouds and sky spinning by over Marcus's shoulder. He tasted leaves and grass and struggled to catch his breath. Thoughts raced through his head—thoughts of having a friend and not having a friend and of Aunt Ernestus's dragons—and of whether Marcus was his own dragon. He seemed to see him spitting fire as he lunged at him, felt the flick of his dragon tail. He whacked Marcus on the side of the head and felt a knee in his stomach.

They rolled apart and lay gasping on the grass, side by side.

"Where do you go to school?" asked Marcus after a while.

Mudge thought for a moment, watching a cloud skim by overhead. "To Woodring. I go to Woodring."

"Do not," said Marcus, jumping up on his knees.

"Do too," said Mudge.

"Do not—do not—do not—" Marcus loomed over him.

"Go there every day," said Mudge, sliding backward and sitting up, leaning against a marble lamb.

"Do not," said Marcus. "You know why you don't—'cause it's all the way on the other side of the city and it would take you all day just to get there. Bet you don't even go to school. Bet you're just . . ."

"Shut up," yelled Mudge. "You just shut up and I do too go to school every day and sometimes Saturdays and Sundays too."

"Where?"

"Here."

"Where here?" asked Marcus, catching his hand in mid-swing.

"Here—there," said Mudge, waving in the direction of the house. "In the gathering room—and Ned's the teacher."

"No fooling," said Marcus, sitting back quickly on the ground.

"Yeah," said Mudge.

"Hey, that's neat." And Marcus sat for a moment and looked at Mudge. "What do you do there?"

"Oh, math and science and book reports and—you know, school stuff."

"Boy—I never heard of having a father for a teacher—is it . . . I mean . . ."

Mudge crossed his legs and plucked at a blade of grass. "Well—with Ned, when he's a teacher he's a teacher and not like he's a father at all—but when he's a father he's still a teacher—if you know what I mean."

Marcus shook his head. "My pop sells bread and tomatoes and milk and stuff—but he's all the time being a father, 'cause if we go in the store looking for M & M's he right away says, 'What're you kids doing here,' or 'Go stack those boxes . . . go do that . . .' But when we leave they're always the M & M's in our pockets."

"I'd like that," said Mudge after a minute. "Having a store and living over it and all."

"Yeah, it's okay. Hey, listen—do you think I could come to your school someday—in the gathering room. I mean, I wouldn't want to have to answer questions and all, but just watch."

"Sure," said Mudge quickly, realizing afterward that he hadn't even stopped to think about it: that he wanted Marcus to come. "I'll ask Ned and tell you when."

They sat for a while cross-legged on the ground, blowing on blades of grass. Mudge remembered why he was there—that he had been on his way to check on Jenkins and the Captain. He wanted to continue on, and he wanted to stay where he was. Wanted to be with Jenkins and with Marcus. He blew a loud bleat on the piece of grass cupped in his hands, and stood up, brushing leaves and sticks and bits of berries off his clothes and out of his hair.

"I've got to go," he said. "Got to do something for Ned—up there."

Marcus got up, too, and for a minute Mudge was afraid he was going to offer to come with him.

"Yeah, me too. Got to go help my pop. But hey, you won't forget about the school—okay?"

"Okay," said Mudge.

"See you." And Marcus ran down the hill toward the gate.

Mudge watched Marcus go, then turned toward Jenkins's place, prepared to find him upset; expecting to see him scurrying around, scolding and shaking his finger.

The ground was freshly tidied: the grass looked as though

it had been swept and there was a small yellow wreath placed squarely in the center of the stone. The row of pinecones was straight and even.

And Jenkins was nowhere in sight.

Mudge waited for a few moments, then started across Edgemount toward the Captain. "It's not like him not to be there," he thought. "I mean, when you think about it—where can he go?"

Mudge picked up a stick and ran it clinkety-clink along a wrought-iron fence. He stopped for a moment to study a crocus nudging the ground, and felt the sun warm against his back. And then continued on.

"Ho, there, my boy. Come and join us," called the Captain from where he sat cross-legged on the ground opposite Jenkins.

Mudge squatted on the ground between them. He felt the early-spring dampness and marveled that the Captain wasn't already complaining of the misery.

"I came because I was wondering, worried some about you guys yesterday. Whether you minded and stuff—all those people. And, Jenkins, the way you like everything just so. Neat like. I was over at your place and it looks terrific, but you must have worked all morning. People shouldn't do that, drop in like that without . . ."

"Oh, it was a splendid day. A splendid day. And I say, Jenkins, you do see why my wreath had to be a little larger, don't you? What with higher rank and all. But the yellow flowers are nice in yours. Fine. Fine."

"Well, sir, I do think they could have been the same, seeing as how you didn't stick around for the battle. Didn't go the distance, as it were."

"Whose fault is that?" said the Captain, rearing back. "I would have been glad to stay. Glad to do my part."

"Yes, yes, but that's all water under the bridge—or over the dam—sir."

"And the speeches—I could have done with a little more. There were some points I would like to have seen covered— my knowledge of firearms, for example."

"And I could have done with a hymn—sir."

"Or something patriotic—stirring and martial, with a beat to it," said the Captain, humming under his breath and tapping his foot.

"It was a fine song that Key fellow wrote—all about 'dawn's early light' and 'bombs bursting in air . . .' "

"*I* never got to hear it," said the Captain, pouting and rubbing his knee. "I would have *liked* to have heard it. Maybe would even have liked to have *sung* it."

"Well, yes, sir. What I mean is, I'm sorry, sir."

"Guess you couldn't sing it now for me, could you?"

"It's the high notes that make it difficult," said Jenkins, clearing his throat.

And Mudge felt as though he were caught in a game of keep-away: as though the ball were flying back and forth over his head—just out of reach.

"O-oh, say, can . . . Oh-oh, say, can you see . . ." Jenkins's voice cracked and he stood up. "Definitely not a sitting-down song—and not much of a song for a bass. Maybe we could try . . ."

"Something else," said the Captain, pulling himself up by a yew.

"Yes, sir," said Jenkins. "How about 'Yankee Doodle'— sir."

Mudge got up and stood for a moment, waiting to see if they would notice him. He felt extra. He backed a few steps away, then turned and stumped down the road, muttering, "What do I care about their dumb old wreaths and their dumb old songs and whose speech was longer. What do I care if their grass gets all trampled down and it takes Jenkins forever to fix it. What do I care . . ."

While from behind him came a ragged but rousing chorus of "Yankee Doodle went to London just to buy a pony . . ."

13

Marcus came every afternoon to Edgemount, arriving after school and after he had gone home to leave his books and gather up a sack of cookies or apples or grapes.

And, for his part, Mudge would hurry through the lessons in the gathering room, prodding Ned along when he digressed, and stopping in the kitchen long enough to pick up some freshly baked bread or a couple of wedges of apple pie. Then he would race along from one part of Edgemount to another, trying to get to see Dorro and Frieda and the Butterfly Lady; Jenkins, the Captain, the Judge, or maybe the Nickersons, before arriving breathless to wait for Marcus on the driveway.

Together they would start up to the gazebo, where they stored the horseshoes and the remains of the kite and an old metal box containing books and scraps of paper and pencil stubs, baseball cards, and old *National Geographics* with tattered covers.

"How come you're always out of breath?" asked Marcus one day when Mudge had come sliding down the road just as Marcus had appeared under the arch. And Mudge remembered how he had had trouble getting away and how Dorro had called him spoil-sport and said that he never had time for her any more and who did he think he was anyway, and he had finally run off and left her standing in front of the stone girl and shaking her fist after him.

"Running," he said, crossing his fingers behind his back. "I've been running."

"How come?" asked Marcus, dropping a large paper bag on the bench that circled the inside of the gazebo.

"It's good for you—for your circulation. Gets the blood stirring, Aunt Ernestus says. What's in the bag?"

Marcus dumped the bag upside down, emptying out a plastic pitcher and a stack of paper cups and packs of Kool-Aid, which slid through the slatted bench onto the floor. "Here—my mom sent it, and we can get water out of that spigot over there and store the packets and cups in the box— and tomorrow's Saturday and I can come pretty much all day and we . . ."

"Might rain," said Mudge, moving back and feeling suddenly crowded.

"That's okay, because what I thought was we could take plastic garbage bags and cut them open and tack them up to keep the rain out—like windows, sort of."

"I don't think so, don't think we could, tack things up, I mean. Don't think Ned would like it."

"Why not?" said Marcus, climbing up and running his finger along the ledge overhead. "Wouldn't hurt anything."

"But Ned would . . ."

"Did you ask him? About me coming to school one day?"

Mudge had asked: Ned had said it was fine. But now Mudge crossed his fingers again and said, "I forgot—but I will—someday."

Marcus locked his fingers over the doorframe and swung forward, letting go and landing in the middle of the floor. "You better had. I've got to go now—just came to bring this stuff and say I couldn't stay. Got to go to the dentist, but I'll be back tomorrow—early. Okay?"

Mudge followed Marcus down the hill and thought about tomorrow and how he had planned to make it up to Dorro and then have a really long visit with the Butterfly Lady and finish the book he hadn't had time to read. He looked hard at the sky and wished that it would rain.

After Marcus left, Mudge doubled back up into Edgemount. He went to see Frieda because he needed cheering up: because he wanted to laugh. He wanted to sit down on an empty flower urn and watch Frieda: listen while the laughter bubbled up from somewhere deep inside of her. He wanted to throw back his head and join in.

He saw her sitting on a rock with her back to him, her shoulders shaking. "Hey, Frieda—tell me something funny. Tell me something . . ."

As Frieda turned around, Mudge saw two fat round tears roll down her cheeks and bounce on her coat. Her body shook convulsively as she said, "I don't think I can today. I've tried and tried. Tried to see something funny—even a little bit funny—but they just weren't nice this time. Not nice at all." And two more tears coursed down her face.

"Who wasn't? What's wrong—Frieda tell me," insisted Mudge.

"I've always tried to be nice when they've come before. Tried not to startle them—stayed in the background—people don't always understand, you know. Even liked the artifacts they've brought, but this was different." She hiccuped, pointing to the bottles and boxes and miles of unwound toilet paper that littered the ground. "And this time," she whispered, leaning close to Mudge, "they had spirits—the kind in bottles, I mean."

"Last night? Were they here last night?" asked Mudge, nudging an empty six-pack with his toe.

"On toward dawn, I'd say. Was light enough to see. They had the ladder again—and some jumped over the wall and . . ." Frieda's voice rose. "They tried to upset the Weeping Woman statue—pulling and tugging from side to side, and toppled the matched urns and . . . and . . . It gives a body an unsettled feeling, I'll tell you that." Frieda took several deep breaths and rearranged her face and patted the damp spots on her chest.

"I've got to go tell Ned," said Mudge, seeing that Frieda was more in control of herself. "He was working over by the pond today. He said to tell him the next time vandals came. He says something's got to be done." Mudge backed away. "But we'll be back. Just leave everything and Ned and I will be right back."

The Judge was standing in the road when Mudge went racing by.

"Whoa there, lad. Where are you off to? The devil after you or what?" He reached his long, white fingers out at Mudge, who swerved to keep from running into him, and landed in a heap almost at his feet.

"Oh—Your Honor, sir. There's a terrible mess over that way, near Frieda's place. The vandals again. And they left a bunch of stuff and tried to turn things over, statues and all, and I'm on my way to tell Ned."

"Dreadful. Dreadful," said the Judge, rubbing his hands together. "Somebody should do something. The city, or the state. Can't have people breaking in here. There are laws—statutes—ought to be upheld—enforced. It's an invasion of privacy. An infringement. An encroachment."

Mudge took a deep breath, ready to run again, and let it all whoosh out as he said, "Hey, Judge—Your Honor, sir, there was this ceremony, for the Captain and Jenkins because they're veterans of the War of 1812 and all, and there were people talking about Historic Preservationists—how they want Edgemount and the gatehouse, our house, made a Historic Site and . . . Well, Your Honor, wouldn't that be an infringement and, and all that other stuff?"

"A Historic Site. Is that what they're saying?" asked the Judge as he walked up and down the road with his hands locked behind his back. "Well, well, well. A Historic Site.

It's about time, I'd say." As he spoke, he swung around to face Mudge. "It is about time."

"But, sir—how about an invasion of privacy? How about . . ."

"Not the same thing at all, lad. It would be a real honor— to be part of a Historic Site. And those of us who are here— finally getting our due: proper recognition. Oh, that is splendid news."

And Mudge turned and ran the rest of the way home.

A telephone-company truck was parked outside the back door, where Aunt Ernestus's car had stood, and from inside the kitchen came a light tapping sound.

"What's that?" said Mudge, stopping beside his father, who was raking the cabbage patch.

"A telephone truck."

"I see what—I guess I mean, *why* is that?"

"We decided, Serena and I, that it might be a good idea to have a phone installed. To keep us from being so cut off— so isolated."

"But we're fine. Not cut off at all," said Mudge.

"And besides, we promised Ernestus before she left. So we could keep in touch," said Ned, turning back to the garden.

"WAIT," screamed Mudge, grabbing hold of the rake. "What's going on? First there was Aunt Ernestus and that dog, then Marcus, and that ceremony for the War of 1812 . . . and all that stuff . . ."

"But Marcus is your friend," said Ned. "And that ceremony was a tribute—an honor—for the veterans of . . ."

"And the vandals and the telephone man," Mudge went on.

"What vandals?" asked Ned, leaning on the rake.

"The vandals at Frieda's place up in the corner. They're back, only worse than usual. They made a terrible mess and shook the statues and upset urns and Frieda's really upset and we've got to *do* something. I promised her."

"You're absolutely right," said Ned, giving Mudge a quick hug. "As soon as the telephone man is finished, we'll call the police."

The telephone man had no sooner gone out of the gate than Ned and Serena were hovering over the telephone. Mudge watched as his mother found the number in the front of the stiff, new phone book. Ned dialed slowly and carefully, and looked—Mudge thought disgustedly—like a child with a toy.

The policeman came in a car with a blue light on top and pulled right into the spot next to the cabbage patch, where the cement was getting a dirty gray color and was already splotched with oil. He asked Ned and Mudge questions and wrote their answers on a little pad of paper. He answered a call on the telephone squawking under the dashboard, and talked about the trouble vandals were causing in the neighborhood. And the next thing Mudge knew, his father was climbing into the front seat of the police car and holding the back door open for him, calling, "Come on, Mudge. We'll ride up and show the officer the damage. Hop in."

Mudge looked at the shiny white car: at the blue domed light on top. He listened to the whine of the radio and thought of the siren lurking somewhere inside. His feet started to inch forward on their own and he had to consciously hold them back. He had to clench his hands behind his back and pretend he was holding on to something—a downspout or a doorjamb—to keep from rushing out and into the car. He had to focus all his thoughts and energies on Frieda waiting up on the hill with the cans and bottles and the hodgepodge trash: had to very deliberately know that he didn't want the policeman and the white car riding through Edgemount: that he wasn't going with them.

And he shook his head and waved them on and held tight to the nonexistent downspout to keep from running after them.

The phone rang twice the next morning during breakfast. The first time it was a wrong number and Mudge said, as Serena came back to the table, "How could it be a wrong number when we just got a number at all?" He glared at the telephone on the wall and thought how much like a black lumpy wart it looked.

Ned took the second call and turned away from the phone laughing. "Kids—playing on the phone. 'Do you have Prince Albert in a can?' " he said in a high voice.

"Well, if you do, you'd better let him out before he suffocates," squeaked Serena back at him. And they both burst out laughing.

"Oh, I see you were the same kind of kid I was," said Ned. "What are some others?"

"My mother used to have a fit," said Serena, wiping her eyes. "How about, 'Is your refrigerator running?'"

"'You'd better catch it,'" said Ned. "And then there was 'Are you the woman who washes,' and when she said no, you said . . ."

"'Oh, you must be awfully dirty then,'" said Ned and Serena together.

Mudge looked from his father to his mother and tried to place them in another time: in other houses with families of their own and doing things he suddenly had no part in. And Serena saw his look and stopped still and watched him for a moment, and then she said, reaching out to him, "Oh, Mudge, there are things that you have missed, aren't there?"

The policeman came back, with another policeman, and stopped to tell Ned they were keeping an eye on the wall for a few nights. "We'll just run up and take a look, so I can show my partner where they're getting in." They stood in the kitchen in their long, black raincoats with hats that came down the backs of their necks and dripped water on the floor. "But don't guess there'll be any trouble in this weather."

They went outside and Mudge heard the splatter of gravel as the police car took off up the road.

14

It had rained all day Saturday and all day Sunday, and Mudge had put on his slicker and slogged through the grounds, visiting Jenkins and the Judge and letting Dorro tell him about what it was like at home and about her father's emporium and the pony kept in the shed at the end of the yard. He made a boat out of twigs, and then another one, and let them race each other down the gully by the side of the road. Twice he went to the arch and looked up the avenue to see if Marcus was coming: half hoping he would— half hoping he would not. And when Marcus didn't come all weekend, Mudge wasn't sure whether he was glad or sorry.

He went to bed early on Sunday night and listened to the rain drumming on the roof overhead. He had a nagging fear that just possibly he had wished so hard that he had made it rain: that maybe it would never stop.

Marcus came early on Monday morning while Mudge was cleaning up the kitchen and Serena had gone off to the store, and Ned sat at the kitchen table drinking coffee and absent-mindedly strumming his guitar.

He stood in the kitchen doorway and called through the screen. "Hey—I didn't think it was ever going to stop raining, and my mom wouldn't let me come, but anyway, we went to a double-feature horror show yesterday and it was okay—and now it's spring—really warm."

"How come—I mean, what are you doing here on a Monday—in the morning and all?" asked Mudge.

Marcus came in, letting the screen door slap shut behind him. "Teachers' meetings."

"And you get a day off? A holiday?" asked Mudge, looking quickly at Ned.

"Morning, Marcus," said Ned. "And don't *you* get any ideas," he added, smiling at Mudge. "No teachers' meetings around here. No holiday today."

"Awww, Ned, come on."

"Hey, neat—you mean you have school today? In the gathering room?" said Marcus, pulling up a chair next to Ned. "Well, since I'm already here, how about I come—if it's okay, I mean."

"It's very okay," said Ned, getting up to refill his cup. "Isn't it, Mudge?"

And Mudge nodded without being really sure. "Except who wants to go to school on a day off anyway?"

"Well, you see, I've got to stick around—out there or

somewhere—cause my mom's coming after a while and bringing the little kids, since it's a day off and all."

"Your mother's coming here?" asked Mudge.

"Not here to your house—but there . . ." And Marcus waved his hand in the direction of Edgemount. "Promised I'd show her the gazebo and everything."

"But why? What for?" asked Mudge.

"Mudge, wait—of course Marcus's family is welcome. Everyone is welcome at Edgemount," said Ned.

"I know that, it's just that . . . just that she never came before."

"Well, if you've really got to know," said Marcus, looking down at the floor. "My mom found out about me coming here and she thought it was kind of, well, you know, strange. All those, you know—and being what it is and all. Well, anyway, she decided she'd better come and have a look, and with everybody off from school, she decided to come today and—and *you know what mothers are like.*"

"Strange . . . why?" asked Mudge, looking around as if seeing things for the very first time.

"Hey—don't get mad or anything. She probably wants to see if it's safe. She's all the time worrying about weirdos and perverts and stuff. And you know what, she'll end up liking it so much I bet she'll keep on coming. Like a park, kind of. Bet she'll bring my Aunt Teresa and my Aunt Joan and . . ."

And Mudge groaned inside himself.

"Anyway, she won't be here until lunchtime—and maybe she'll bring something to eat. And she wants to meet you and . . ."

"And now it's time to get to work," said Ned, standing up. "Come on, boys—no holiday in this school today."

At first Mudge felt self-conscious, sitting at the table in the gathering room while Ned talked about lichens and how there were hundreds of known kinds and how they usually grow only a few millimeters a decade—as though it were all the most exciting thing in the world. He looked at the pictures Ned held, then over his shoulder at Marcus, and back at the pictures again.

Ned put the science book away and got out his copy of *Uncle Tom's Cabin*, turning to Mudge. "Well, how's it coming, Mudge. Have you gotten far enough along to see if there's any relation between the book and the Fugitive Slave Law of 1850 . . ."

"Hey, I've heard of that. The book, I mean," said Marcus, pulling his chair up to the table. "My teacher's talked about it in school—that's the one about that guy Simon Legree—right?"

"Right," said Ned. "It's an anti-slavery novel by Harriet Beecher Stowe. Have you had a chance to read it?"

"Well, no. We could read it—for extra credit—but we didn't have to. But I might someday."

"Would you like mine?" asked Ned, pushing the book across the table. "You could take it home and get started on it, if you'd like."

"Hey, thanks. Okay—and I'll take care of it," said Marcus, turning the book over in his hands.

Ned talked for a while about who Harriet Beecher Stowe was and why she wrote the book and how when President Lincoln met her he said, "So this is the little lady who wrote the book that made this great war." He talked about Topsy and Little Eva and what it meant to be called an "Uncle Tom." He talked about all the things that Mudge already knew—and he knew that Ned was doing it for Marcus. And Marcus sat watching Ned and holding on to the book.

"I've got to go," said Marcus when the lesson was over. "Got to go find my mom and the kids before they get lost. You coming?" he asked Mudge.

"Yeah, in a minute," said Mudge, hooking his feet around the legs of the chair. "I have to do this spelling test and— I'll find you . . ."

Ned went to the door and held it open for Marcus. "Come again—and tell me how you like the book."

"Yeah, okay. Yes, sir, I will. And you," he called across to Mudge, "you'd better come. My mom doesn't think you even exist. See you."

When the doorbell rang in the gathering room, Mudge thought that Marcus had come back; that he had forgotten something.

"What're you doing back?" he called as he swung open the door, gasping at the man and woman standing on the step.

"Oh, good morning, good morning. Yes, I *am* back again . . ." And Mudge recognized the man with the umbrella who had conducted the ceremonies the week before.

"I'm sorry—my son thought it was someone else," said Ned, who had come up behind Mudge. "May I help you?"

"Well, yes. I'm Frederick Hooper from the General Society of the War of 1812. And this is Miss Duckett, our scribe."

Ned started to speak: to introduce Mudge and himself: but Mr. Hooper went on.

"We were here last Sunday—for our little ceremonies, you know—except Miss Duckett here, who had the flu. So I volunteered to bring her back. As the scribe, it is her duty to write up the event—to describe the setting—the graves and the markers."

Miss Duckett waved a pencil and a notebook as if to lend substance to what he was saying.

"And I thought that while she was here there might be some other monuments she could look at—those of particular interest. We don't like to trouble you, but if you could just point out a few, head us in the right direction, as it were."

"Oh, I'll do better than that," said Ned, winking at Mudge. "I'll lend you my son. Mudge knows all there is to know about Edgemount. Knows it inside and out. He'll be glad to take you around, won't you, Mudge? But perhaps you'd better move your car out of the driveway—there's a spot around back by the cabbage patch. If you don't mind . . ."

"But, Ned," said Mudge, when Mr. Hooper had gone to move his car. "What about Marcus? I have to meet him."

"I don't think it will take long," said Ned. "A quick tour, just to get them started. Then you can meet Marcus. Okay?"

Mudge fretted along behind Mr. Hooper and Miss Duckett and wondered why they weren't tired. He had taken them up by the gazebo and down by the rose garden. He had shown them the oldest markers at Edgemount and waited while Miss Duckett copied inscriptions into her notebook. He had held sticker bushes back while she crawled around the ground, trying to recapture words that were being swallowed up by dirt and moss. Now he pointed the way up around the pond toward the Captain's place and listened halfheartedly while Mr. Hooper went on about Edgemount being "a veritable haven, a place of solace in the hubbub of every day. It's a sanctuary, a refuge."

"Some haven," thought Mudge, catching sight of a police car rounding a curve and heading for the gate. "Some refuge . . . some sanctuary." He kicked a stone and watched it skitter past Mr. Hooper.

"Aha—here we are," said Mr. Hooper, hoisting the umbrella higher under his arm. "This is where we had our first ceremony—and there's the wreath. One of our very own veterans." He turned to Miss Duckett and swung his arm vaguely in the direction of the Captain, who was crouching behind an obelisk. Mudge caught his breath and held it, but Mr. Hooper continued. "Buried here in 1814—and over there—farther along . . ."

"Psst, my boy." The Captain darted behind a pine tree and whispered to Mudge. "The flowers are ruined—they were fading around the edges, and then the deluge. Perhaps they could do something. Replace them. You ask them, my boy."

"I can't do that," said Mudge quickly.

"Oh, you poor dear," said Miss Duckett, swooping toward him. "You must be getting tired."

"No, ma'am. No—I'm fine. Honest."

"Tell her about the flowers. And maybe for next year . . ." The Captain hurried around behind Mudge.

"The flowers were fine. Fresh and . . ."

"Yes indeed they were, though I must confess they've seen better days," said Mr. Hooper, nodding his head. "But I think Miss Duckett is right. We've worn you out. I do think we can continue on our own and you just run along now. We really appreciate your help, your time." And they started down the road in the direction of Jenkins, and Mudge heard Mr. Hooper saying ". . . right over this way . . . name of Jenkins . . . aide-de-camp . . ."

"But you didn't tell them about the flowers—that next year I'd like . . ." said the Captain.

"About time you got here," said Marcus when Mudge got to the gazebo.

"These people came that needed showing around and Ned said it would only take a minute and it took forever and they wanted to see everything." Mudge decided not to tell Marcus that Mr. Hooper was the man with the umbrella who had come before. He looked around and suddenly the gazebo seemed filled with people. Someone had spread a blanket on the floor and three boys and a little girl were eating sandwiches out of waxed paper and poking one another. Another little girl sat in a stroller drinking cherry Kool-Aid out of a paper cup that she had squashed almost in half. A woman sat on the bench sorting cookies into piles.

"This is my mom," said Marcus. "And she's brought you lunch and you didn't come and ..."

"Marcus—stop that. He had to help his father. Just what he ought to do. Hello, Mudge, I'm glad to meet you at last. Been hearing a lot, from Marcus here." She stood up and held her hand out to Mudge and he liked the way it felt— sure and gentle all at the same time.

Marcus's mother rummaged in her paper shopping bag, pulling out a handful of sandwiches and holding them out to Mudge. "Here—there's tuna, or egg salad, and here's one bologna left. Sit down. Sit down."

"Can I have another?"

"I want a cookie ..."

"He hit me ..."

Voices stuck to Mudge like burrs.

"I don't like tuna fish," the little girl said, coming to stand next to Marcus. "This is Jenny," he said to Mudge. "And the one in the stroller is Christine. And they're Tony and Joseph and Paul . . . I'm the oldest," said Marcus proudly.

And Mudge ate one sandwich, and then another, and split an egg salad with Tony, who turned out to be only a year younger than Marcus. He drank Kool-Aid and let Christine climb up on his lap after she got tired of crawling around the floor. He thought about the gazebo that had been his, and then his and Marcus's, and was now suddenly filled with people. He took the cookie Jenny handed him and looked around at the clutter in the gazebo and thought that it looked like Frieda's place after the vandals had been there. Suddenly he wanted to be part of the gazebo himself—and to move back and watch from the benches that rimmed the outside. He wondered what Marcus's house looked like—and weighed it against the order of the gatehouse.

He helped Marcus and Tony clean up, picking up paper cups and lollipop sticks and chasing waxed-paper wrappers as they were caught in the breeze. He watched while Marcus's mother hoisted Jenny up on her hip and Marcus pushed Christine in the stroller, and Tony and Joseph and Paul went behind, carrying the shopping bag and the blanket and the Kool-Aid jug—and together they all went down the hill. He started to follow them, and then turned back, saying that he had a chore to do and waving goodbye.

Mudge sat in the empty gazebo and the silence seemed that much greater because of their going. He watched a Kool-Aid stain drying from the edges in and gathered up one remaining piece of paper tucked under the bench, and headed along toward the vaults.

Mudge had to wait a while to get the Nickersons' attention, and when he got it, they didn't pay him much mind. The vaults seemed filled with a murmur of voices: chatting, gossiping, and calling back and forth—and for a minute he thought he was back in the gazebo with Marcus and his family.

Just when he was about to move on, a voice he thought belonged to Sarah called out to him. "You talk about crowded —you don't know the meaning of the word. Up here in the vaults . . ."

"And besides," said Uncle William Nickerson, "Aunt Ernestus and Thanatos have moved on. Shouldn't be too crowded at your place."

Mudge paused, sure that he had never told the Nickersons about Aunt Ernestus's dog: about Thanatos. "But there are people coming all the time now," he said. "Vandals and policemen, and now Marcus's mother and all those children."

"Ah, yes, the children," said Beloved Angeline. "Talk about crowding—got so bad around here we sent some of the cousins over to visit the Butterfly Lady. Oh, listen, here they come now. Seems they've learned another recitation."

And Mudge heard a chorus of voices coming closer and closer, saying, "The Raven—by Edgar Allan Poe. 'Once upon a midnight dreary, while I pondered weak and weary . . .'"

Back at the house, the phone was ringing. "Slipcovers—somebody selling slipcovers this time," said Serena, replacing the receiver. Mudge glared at the phone for a minute, then stuck his tongue out at it and turned away.

Serena and Ned were playing their guitars. They played "Frog Went A'courtin'," and sang alternating verses.

And in the middle of the third verse Aunt Ernestus called to see if everything was all right.

15

After a while Mudge began to get used to things—but in the way that he once got used to a stiff new shoe that wore a blister on his heel. Rub, scrape, rub, scrape, rub . . . But unlike the shoe, he could not kick this new way of life off. He gradually got used to the ringing of the phone and the occasional letter from Aunt Ernestus; to Marcus's mother coming sometimes on a long spring evening and walking slowly through Edgemount with the younger children tumbling around her, and even once or twice to Tony tagging behind Marcus and him. He got so he scarcely noticed the police car as it made a quick tour of the grounds—and once he caught himself waving to the policeman in the car.

But one Saturday morning a reporter came to Edgemount, bringing a photographer with him. He knocked on the door, and by the time Serena had answered it, the photographer was already at work. She shot pictures of the black iron gates and the wall and the gatehouse itself; of the underside of the arch that spanned the driveway, and the door of the greater part of the house, and of the gathering room as well.

She came to stand behind the reporter, so that together they formed a kind of phalanx, elbowing their way inside when Serena opened the door.

"I'm Bob Ames from the *Herald*," the reporter said. "Mind if we get some inside shots? The house is of particular interest to our readers, to citizens everywhere. A piece of the past that is now going to be preserved. A real plus for the city—for everyone interested in the preservation of history."

The girl with the camera took pictures of the living room and the window glass that was thick and whorled; of the entrance to the hallway, lined on both sides with Ned's books.

And Mudge, pressed silently against the fireplace, knew that the invasion had come to Edgemount. He saw Ned looking tight-lipped and pale, standing in the doorway, and knew that his father knew it, too.

"Now just a minute. You can't come in here like this. What's this all about?" Ned forced himself out into the center of the room.

"You mean you don't know—haven't heard?" Bob Ames turned to the photographer and shrugged his shoulders. "Well then, maybe we should wait—Erin and I. Though of course a story will be inevitable. May as well let us continue on now, right?" And he nodded imperceptibly to Erin.

"Wrong," said Ned, holding up his hand. "What are you telling us?"

"A call came into the *Herald* office this morning from the Society for the Preservation of Historical Sites. The funding has gone through, the money raised, and as I'm sure you know, that was the only thing holding up the acquisition of

Edgemount. It is now ready to be declared a Historic Site. Now, if you could just give us some facts, some background . . ."

"Not right now," said Ned, shepherding them to the door. "It's not an appropriate time. A little bit of a shock, though of course we knew it was coming . . . Expected it, even."

Serena pulled Mudge toward her and squeezed his shoulder.

"Might be a human-interest angle here," said the reporter on his way out the door. "How does it feel to be suddenly uprooted? To have your house yanked out from under you? To be caretakers with nothing to care for? How about some pictures of you and the family?"

Mudge heard the door slam as he darted into the kitchen.

The news came officially by registered letter, arriving later in the morning. The letter was from the Board of Trustees of Edgemount and told of money that had been raised through endowments and trust funds. Edgemount Cemetery and its existing gatehouse was declared a Historic Site. The letter spoke of practical matters: of the committee that was anxious to get into the house—anxious to begin restoration and preservation: of a need to have the house vacant as soon as possible: of severance pay.

Mudge felt mired down in silence. As though it oozed up around him, muffling sound and catching and holding him so that he could not budge. Serena moved quietly around the kitchen, putting out bread and cheese and meat for sandwiches, then putting the uneaten food back in the refrigerator. Ned sat with his head in his hands. When Mudge saw Marcus at the back door, he felt as though he had to struggle physically to free himself: as though his legs were weak with disuse.

"Come on," he said, pushing against Marcus on the porch and moving up the road—slowly at first, then faster and faster, until Marcus had to run to keep up with him.

"Hey, wait up. What's the matter?" puffed Marcus, catching up and grabbing hold of Mudge's sleeve.

But still Mudge ran on, until he couldn't run any farther; until he collapsed in a heap on the far side of a mausoleum mossed along one side. He leaned back against the cool stone, gasping for breath and holding his side.

"Okay—what's eating you?" asked Marcus, flopping down next to him.

Mudge dropped his head on his knees and listened to the thudding of his heart. "They did it," he said after a while. "They won."

"Who did? Did what? Your folks, you mean?"

"No. No. Did it *to* them. To Serena and Ned." Mudge raised his head and felt the sweat drying cold on his face. "The Historic Preservationists, and now we have to move and . . ."

"Move?" yelled Marcus. "How can you move when I just got to know you. Tell them you won't . . . tell them . . . What are Historic Preservationists, anyway?"

"People who preserve things. Old stuff—houses and estates

—and graveyards like Edgemount. Turn them into Historic Sites, sort of, and take care of them and people can come see them and all."

"But you guys do that. Take care of this place, and we come here, and my mom, and pop wants to come too someday, and other people could too. We could put up signs. We could . . ."

"It's not the same, I don't think. They have committees and things, and the newspapers were here. They—the Preservationists—have been trying to raise money and now they have enough and—and—we've got to go . . . Somewhere."

"Just don't. Tell them it's your place—your house."

"But that's the point," said Mudge, feeling suddenly like Serena; mouthing Serena's words. "It's not ours. It's always just been . . . was never meant to be permanent. We knew when we came here—well, Serena and Ned did—have known it all along."

"What'd you come for, then," said Marcus, kicking angrily at the corner of the mausoleum. "What'd you come here for in the first place, I want to know."

"Because, because of . . ." And Mudge stopped short, knowing somehow that he couldn't tell Marcus about Ned's friend the governor and how he had been killed and how much Ned had cared and how for a time he couldn't do anything at all: how Serena had had to bring them here.

"How come, I said," asked Marcus angrily. "How come? How come? How come?"

"I don't know," said Mudge, getting up slowly. "They

just did—Ned and Serena. How do I know—I was just a little kid, for pete's sake."

He started home, thinking about Ned sitting with his
head in his hands and Serena moving quietly around the
kitchen. And Mudge wanted to be with them: needed to be
there. And somewhere inside of him, and far away, a very
small thought began to stir.

"Hey," yelled Marcus after him. "What about the gazebo?
What'll they do with the gazebo?"

Ned and Serena were still in the kitchen: as though time
had stopped: as though it were ready to start again when
Mudge came through the door.

The phone shrilled, and shrilled again. It was a reporter,
and another one. The doorbell rang and it was a committee
of men and women, some from the other day—hesitant and
apologetic. They didn't mean to be premature; didn't mean
to intrude: but if they could just have a quick look around.
They had waited so long to see the house. And Serena had to
ask them to come another day.

After a while Ned stood up, pushing his chair back. "Well,
we knew it was coming," he said. "Now it's just a matter of
getting ourselves together—deciding what to do."

But in the days that followed, deciding what to do seemed
to be the one thing that nobody was able to do.

There were long and dwindling conversations between Ned and Serena that started at breakfast and went on after Mudge was in bed at night. The words "maybe" . . . "suppose" . . . "could we" tightened around them like a cocoon.

Serena went out to the store and came back with newspapers—both local and out of town—and together she and Ned sat at the kitchen table and circled help-wanted ads. They made up lists of people they knew: contacts: job possibilities. Ned wrote letters and tore them up—and wrote other letters. He called people on the phone.

"The best jobs all seem to be out of town," said Ned. "It would mean going back where we came from. Have to set up interviews." And he looked at the calendar and shook his head.

"If only I could go with you," said Serena, looking at the list. "Make one trip and see everyone there is to see, look for a place to live."

Mudge saw his father's eyes brighten, then darken suddenly: as though Serena had thrown him a life line and he had almost caught it. "No—no. We can't. You have to stay here at Edgemount. After all, there's Mudge, and we are still in charge here until . . ."

And then the "maybes" and the "supposes" and the "could we's" started all over again. Ned talked about going back into the law firm, and about teaching, and working for legal aid. He talked about apartments and houses; about buying and renting. Sometimes he sat with his head in his hands and sometimes he went out, letting the door slam behind him, and Mudge would see him striding up the road into Edgemount.

"It all happened a little bit too soon," said Serena to Mudge one afternoon when Ned had gone out to trim the hedges. "If only we could have had a little more time here. It was all going so well—especially after the visit from Ernestus." Serena was going through the kitchen cabinets, sorting cans and boxes and bottles; throwing away old jelly glasses and broken saucers. Mudge sensed an impatience about her: as if she wanted to bundle everything up and start off with it. As if she were through marking time. "A little more time and he would have done it on his own. He knew we had stayed here long enough—for you and me—even for himself. You know what it's like, Mudge?" Serena sat on the top of the ladder, holding a copper mold in the shape of a fish. "It's as though Ned has gotten to the end of the high diving board and isn't able to jump."

Mudge had a fleeting picture of Ned with his guitar and his books and his hedge trimmer teetering on the end of the diving board while the water rippled beneath him. And Mudge felt a pain in the middle of his stomach.

Since the day the reporter came, Mudge had avoided the grounds of Edgemount. He stayed home with Serena and Ned and the "maybes" and the "supposes": all the time wanting to hold his ears, yet knowing somehow that he had to listen.

Over and over he saw the picture of Ned balanced on the end of the high dive—and one Mudge wanted to take hold of his father's hand, telling him everything would be all right, while another Mudge wanted to run up behind him and push.

Mudge wanted to stay at Edgemount forever, yet somehow he understood Serena's restlessness as she sorted her way through first one cupboard and then another. Understood how she was ready to move on.

He wanted to see his friends: to see the Butterfly Lady and Frieda and the others and tell them what had happened —what was going to happen. But he was angry at them. As if in some way they had gone on and he had stopped: as if they had betrayed him. He wanted to see Marcus but avoided him: and when he did see him they were awkward with one another—as though they were in each other's way.

But, most of all, he felt as though he had Marcus's kite and was running with it into the wind: only it wasn't going anywhere.

It was as though something outside Mudge knew what he had to do before he did it. He got up one morning with a certainty that hurt all the way down inside of him. With a sureness that made his teeth ache.

He did lessons in the gathering room and weeded the cabbage patch and helped Serena in the kitchen, all the while knowing that something was going to happen. And as the afternoon wore along and the day took on that special brightness of spring, something grew and grew inside him until he knew what that something was. And the knowing scared him some.

Ned and Serena went to take a walk up on the hill and Mudge waited alone at the kitchen table. He was afraid and he forced himself to think of something safe: of cold winter nights in the gathering room: of his mother and father singing and playing their guitars: of the newfound sureness of Marcus—and even Aunt Ernestus. But the safe pictures gradually receded and he felt at the edge of things.

The telephone bulged on the wall: black and ugly and warty-looking. It seemed to throb: to reach out and grab at him. It grew and grew until everything around him seemed ready to burst and Mudge felt his feet carry him across the kitchen; his fingers struggling to dial and not to dial.

He felt the house shake beneath him as the phone was picked up on the other end and he heard himself saying, "Aunt Ernestus, this is Mudge. The dragons have come to Edgemount—and Ned needs you—we all need you to come . . ."

16

Mudge stood at the door of the gathering room and watched as the taxi pulled away. He waited there until it turned into the avenue and was swallowed up in traffic—and Ned and Serena swallowed up with it. Then he went back inside to the schoolbooks waiting on the table and Aunt Ernestus with a page of math problems in front of her, and Thanatos lying quietly on the floor. It was as though the gathering room had accepted Aunt Ernestus: as though the men and women from time past moved quietly and freely. And in a way that Mudge didn't fully understand, they seemed to be stepping back: receding.

Mudge did his fractions in a haphazard way—crossing out and splotching and erasing—as though he struggled against the acceptance of the room. And without looking at Aunt Ernestus he let his eyes skim the mourners' bench and the wood stove and the window seat where they had hidden *At the Back of the North Wind.* He saw the guitars and Serena's desk and the plat that showed Edgemount divided into sections and the sections into lots. Already the things in the room had a once-removed feeling, as though they were not as familiar as they had been. And Mudge knew that somehow he had set things in motion: that now something was going to happen.

He rubbed a hole in his paper and tried to patch it with spit. He thought about how Aunt Ernestus had come, arriving the morning after his call, and coming into the house as if she had just left it a few minutes before.

He remembered how she had motioned for Thanatos to follow her and how she had unpacked his bowls and kibble, saying, "I read in the paper about what's happened to Edgemount and I thought maybe there might be something I could do. And seeing as I'm in-between cases—had some time . . . You must want to make plans, see about jobs . . . a place to live. If I could stay here—Mudge and I—and keep things going . . ." And she said all this without once looking at Mudge.

Mudge had watched his father: had seen Ned start to bristle and to clench and unclench his hands. After a while, he had seen Ned spread his hands out flat on the table and lean back in his chair and say, "Yes, Ernestus—I think, I think . . . I think we need you here . . . I think it will work out."

Serena had looked hard at Mudge; and Mudge had looked down at his shoes and at the water dripping in the sink and at the forsythia branch outside the kitchen window.

There had been more talk around the kitchen table, with Aunt Ernestus listening carefully and Mudge holding on to the sides of his chair as if that might keep things from happening. There were lists that were narrowed down, and decisions that were made; and Mudge heard a firmness in his father's voice that he had seldom heard before: saw that Serena's hands were quiet, no longer restless.

The clock struck and Mudge wriggled in his chair. He looked up and saw Marcus watching him through the screen door and waved him inside.

"Hey—I've got your father's book," he said, holding out *Uncle Tom's Cabin* and stopping when he saw Aunt Ernestus.

"This is Marcus," said Mudge, pushing his paper away and standing up. And turning to Marcus: "This is Aunt Ernestus. You know—I told you about her . . ."

"Oh, yeah, well—hi," said Marcus, dropping the book on the table. "I've heard of you—I mean, he's told me about you. And I'm glad to meet you and all."

"Oh, that's lovely, lovely," said Aunt Ernestus. "To meet one of Mudge's friends. Such a good boy, and just like his father . . . and now we're here together—in charge of things."

And Mudge and Marcus looked at one another and rolled their eyes up into their heads.

"Now, can you come over to the kitchen?" Aunt Ernestus went on sweeping pencils and papers off the table and putting them away. "I've made brownies and we'll have milk and . . ."

"Well, I would if I could, except my pop'll let me have it if I'm not right back to help him unload the cartons. But my mom told me I had to get this book back before the kids got hold of it. One time my brother Paul ate all the edges off

a library book and we had to pay and . . . Brownies—
wow . . ."

"I'll tell you what," said Aunt Ernestus, shepherding the
boys out the door. "I'll give you one and you can eat it on
the way home. How about that?"

After Marcus had gone off, Mudge finished the last of his
milk and washed the plate and glass and put them away.
Aunt Ernestus wiped the kitchen table, zigzagging back and
forth with the dishrag and cupping her hand at the edge to
catch the nonexistent crumbs. She swept the floor and
straightened the dish towels on the rack and watered the
plants that Mudge had seen Serena water that morning.

Her very busyness made Mudge feel as though he had
sprouted an extra set of hands, and he shifted from foot to
foot and wondered what to do next. He went to empty the
trash and found the can already empty and neatly lined with
a paper bag. He opened the refrigerator and stood leaning
on the door and looking inside. He heard the rattle of dishes
in back of him and turned away from the blank-faced stare
of milk bottles and ketchup and pickle jars to see Aunt
Ernestus setting the table for supper.

"Well, I believe in getting things over with," she said.
"Now that's done and . . ."

And Mudge looked at the two blue willow plates face to
face across the table and knew with a certainty that he and
Aunt Ernestus were alone together: that something had
ended: that something terribly new was about to begin.

"Now let's . . ."

"When will . . ."

Mudge and Aunt Ernestus spoke at the same time, their voices locking and crashing against the edges of the silent room.

"Now let's go and see to things outside," said Aunt Ernestus, taking off her apron and folding it over the back of a chair. "Your father told me to keep an eye on things, but I'll have to count on you to tell me if things are as they should be. There's just time before I have to start supper."

They went up the hill, walking side by side, with Thanatos running out in front, chasing birds and leaves and the very idea of chasing things.

Mudge saw Dorro squatting next to the statue of the stone girl, waving and pointing and gesturing to him. He stooped down, pretending to tie his shoe, and let Aunt Ernestus and Thanatos go ahead.

Dorro landed with a thud on the ground next to him and toppled forward. "Well," she said, righting herself. "She did come, didn't she?"

"Who did?"

"Her—what's her name . . ."

"Aunt Ernestus—and you know her name," said Mudge.

"Aunt Ernestus—and you know who I meant," said Dorro. "But anyway, she did come when you called her because you thought Ned was going backward instead of forward. And coming counts for something, too. My papa used to say that's what family was for. Hey, look," said Dorro, pointing in the direction of the pond. "She's got a good arm—look."

And Mudge watched while Aunt Ernestus skipped a stone so that it skimmed its way to the other side of the pond, barely rippling the water beneath it.

"Come on," said Dorro, starting forward. "Let's go watch." And Mudge held back for a minute, then ran to catch up with Dorro. They stood one on either side of Aunt Ernestus, watching silently. After a while, Mudge picked up a stone and sent it out onto the pond with a great splashing and churning of water. He heard Dorro laugh out loud.

"No, look, Mudge," said Aunt Ernestus, turning to him. "Like this, and you need a smaller stone, and flat. I taught your father to do this years ago."

Mudge sent the next stone out over the water.

"There, that's better," said Aunt Ernestus, neatly firing off another stone. "You know something, Mudge? I'm beginning to understand now why Ned had to come here—what it was that this place gave to him, just as I think you understand why he has to move on—to go forward. Would have to, even if things hadn't happened."

"Yes—but where?" asked Mudge, dropping his handful of stones all at once. "Where do you think we'll end up? What will happen to us?"

Aunt Ernestus rubbed a round pink stone back and forth between her hands and looked out over the water. "I'm not really sure—it's up to your father and your mother, though the way it looks now, I'll bet that Ned is leaning toward that job in legal aid, going back to the city where you lived before."

"How come?" asked Mudge.

"Well," said Aunt Ernestus, sending off another stone and waiting for the ripples in the water to disappear. "Probably it's because Ned knows that sometimes we have to go back . . . to piece things together and pick up where we were and then continue on. And also, I think that all things considered, Ned finds that that's what interests him the most. He can use his legal training and—despite the impression he sometimes gives—your father is a very caring person. And there is more for Serena—opportunities and . . ."

"But it won't be . . ."

"And as to what will happen to you—good things, Mudge. Good things. Remember, it will still be you and Ned and Serena, and that's what counts."

"Yeah," called Dorro over her shoulder as she headed back to the statue. "My papa always said, 'Home Is Where The Heart Is.' He liked it so much he had Mama embroider it on a sampler in pink and yellow thread, with flowers on it, and hang it in the parlor next to the melodeon."

And Mudge watched as Dorro climbed up on the monument and stood tiptoe to measure herself against the stone girl in the ruffled dress.

"Ho there, my boy," the Captain called as they passed his way. "The wreath is gone—the flowers died and shriveled and the rains came . . . Your father took it away. I would have liked to keep it a little longer . . . would like another one. Where are you off to? I'll walk along. It's been a while since we've seen you . . . had to carry my own messages—in fact, I'm on my way to find Jenkins right now . . . find that a little exercise is good for the misery." And the Captain hurried out in front, still talking, and leaving Mudge behind.

A stirring of voices came from the road that led to the vaults, and Mudge watched as Thanatos held his head up and looked sharply ahead of him.

"Oh, we do hate goodbyes . . . just refuse to say them, but you will come back, won't you . . . for a visit . . ."

"Anytime . . ." said Sarah.

"We're always here," called the rest of the Nickersons.

And the wind ruffled the trees overhead.

"You know something, Mudge," said Aunt Ernestus when he had caught up with her. "We don't exactly leave things behind, you know." She stooped to pick up a piece of paper from the side of the road and then went on. "We always take a bit of everything with us—and everybody, too. But then we leave bits and pieces of ourselves—and that's the hard part. It tears at us." And the corners of her mouth twitched as she remembered a lifetime of taking—and leaving behind.

Mudge stood looking up at the white underside of leaves. "Aunt Ernestus," he said, stopping in the middle of the path. "Aunt Ernestus, there's something I've . . . something I've wanted to know . . ."

Aunt Ernestus stopped beside him and waited.

"A long time ago, when I was little and Ned's friend the governor was killed and we all left—just up and left and came here . . . Didn't it hurt awfully?" And Mudge felt in a sudden rush that he had been disloyal to his father by asking the question. But he let the question hang and waited for Aunt Ernestus to answer it.

Aunt Ernestus waited a long, long time. She walked a few steps forward by herself, then turned and came back to where Mudge still stood. "Oh my, yes, Mudge. It hurt awfully. But there are things that hurt more—at least, to my way of thinking. Like grudges . . . and not letting ourselves understand . . ." Aunt Ernestus and Mudge moved slowly forward. "You see—with our friends, and the best sense of family is that they are our friends, sometimes we have to accept things simply because they *are* our friends. We have to care enough . . ."

"Dorro told me once that it's the caring that matters," said Mudge.

"She's right, this Dorro person," said Aunt Ernestus, reaching out and lightly fingering a leaf. "But the thing about caring is that you have to be willing to let yourself be hurt—sometimes over and over and over again. But that's only one side of it, Mudge. And the other . . . the other side is that glorious, soaring bursting-at-the-seams kind of something that makes it all worthwhile. Over and over and over again."

Aunt Ernestus's plain, flat, everyday kind of a face broke into hundreds of lines and folds and creases and Mudge thought that its sudden crinkling let a light shine through that seemed to come from some place deep inside her. And Mudge wondered how he had ever thought he couldn't remember what she looked like. He closed his eyes and opened them—as if trying to memorize something, then swung into step beside Aunt Ernestus, and as they walked, their sleeves brushed lightly against one another's.

Mudge saw the Judge pacing back and forth by the side of the road. His first thought was to duck past while he was facing the other way. But he knew there was something he had to tell him.

"Your Honor, sir," called Mudge, darting off to the side while Aunt Ernestus continued on ahead. "About the Historic Preservationists—they got what they wanted. What you wanted. And Edgemount is going to be a Historic Site. It was in the newspapers and everything. I just wanted to let you know."

"Oh, we know. We know. We all know, lad. And we're . . . I must say, it makes us proud, except I understand there will be changes . . . That you and Ned and Serena . . . And we're sorry about that." The Judge's voice grew suddenly gruff and he turned and paced in the other direction.

Mudge felt better after he had seen Frieda. She sat on the righted flower urn and laughed and laughed, rocking back and forth and telling Mudge about the policemen who came and the vandals who didn't come any more. She watched Aunt Ernestus, who had stopped by a mound of pachysandra and was pulling weeds, and called to Thanatos, who looked the other way. And Frieda laughed.

As they started up the hill, Mudge heard the sound of singing and he looked through the bushes, full now, and green, and saw Jenkins and the Captain. They stood side by side, arms across each other's shoulders, their uniforms looking pale and faded, and sang "The Star Spangled Banner." Mudge stood for a moment and watched, then he slipped past and led the way to the gazebo.

He leaned back on the green-painted bench and looked around the gazebo: at the metal box still shoved under the seat, filled with papers and pencil stubs and *National Geographics* with tattered covers; at the empty plastic pitcher lying on the seat, and the stains on the floor of dried Kool-Aid and flattened M & M's.

"We came here a lot, Marcus and I," said Mudge, looking out over the city. "He lives out there somewhere—and he asked me to come sometime and I . . . I tried, but I . . ." And Mudge remembered the cars and fire trucks, the motorcycles and the people that were Silver Street. He sat up straight. "But I would now. Would go . . . if you thought there was time . . ."

"I'm sure there's time," said Aunt Ernestus, picking up a

baseball card off the floor and handing it to Mudge. "What-ever happens, there'll be time enough for that."

Aunt Ernestus stood up and walked around the inside of the gazebo, her fingers trailing against the weathered wood. "You know, Mudge—that may be the hardest part—leaving Marcus. But don't ever forget—it's something to have had a friend. And I know as well as I know anything at all that there will be other friends. There will be others."

The Butterfly Lady was rubbing the iron butterfly with hy-drangea leaves when Mudge and Aunt Ernestus stopped by.

"Good—you've come," she said, opening her arms wide to Mudge. "I was afraid you wouldn't. Would just . . . Say, how does it look? The butterfly, I mean. I've taken to shining it. Sometimes people come and . . ."

Mudge felt a strange tightening in his throat. He held on to one of the butterfly wings and couldn't think of anything to say.

"Remember, Mudge," said the Butterfly Lady, looking away from him. "Remember, when things get rough, there are always the recitations." And she stepped back several paces and began to speak:

It was many and many a year ago,
In a kingdom by the sea,
That a maiden there lived whom you may know
By the name of Annabel Lee . . .

Her voice grew lighter and faded away and Mudge turned.

*And this maiden she lived with no other thought
Than to love and be loved by me,*

finished Aunt Ernestus, as together she and Mudge started down the hill toward the house.

They are all together now in Aunt Ernestus's car, with Ned and Serena and Thanatos in back; with Aunt Ernestus and Mudge up front.

As they start down the driveway, Mudge looks back over his shoulder. The shades on the street side of the house are up. The windows are open.

The past music and the laughter from the gathering room and the noise of the workmen tumble onto the outside and mix with the city sounds: of buses and taxis and children playing in the street.

And in the background can be heard the voices of Mudge and Ned and Serena; of Marcus and Aunt Ernestus; of the man with the umbrella and the reporter and the members of the committee.

There are the sounds of living; of endings and, always, of new beginnings. There are the sounds of the little bits of Edgemount that Mudge is taking with him: of the parts that he is leaving behind.

And further in the background, heard only by Mudge—

and perhaps, because of the way she smiles and tilts her head, by Aunt Ernestus—are the voices of Dorro and the Butterfly Lady, the Captain, Jenkins, Frieda; the Judge and all the Nickersons.

As the car turns out of Edgemount and into the avenue, as it reaches the corner of Silver Street, there is Marcus standing on the curb. He waves, and Mudge waves, until they cannot see each other any longer.

And Mudge turns and looks out the window at the city stretching ahead of him.